Spirits & Wine

Spirits & Wine

Susan Newhof

The University of Michigan Press ❧ *Ann Arbor*

Published in the United States of America by
The University of Michigan Press
Manufactured in the United States of America
♾ Printed on acid-free paper

2014   2013   2012   2011   4   3   2   1

A CIP catalog record for this book is available from the British Library.

Library of Congress Cataloging-in-Publication Data

Newhof, Susan J., 1952–
        Spirits and wine / Susan Newhof.
            p. cm.
        ISBN 978-0-472-11800-7 (cloth : alk. paper) — ISBN 978-0-472-
02803-0 (e-book)
        1. Middle-aged persons—Fiction.   2. Married people—Fiction.
3. Ghosts—Michigan—Fiction.   4. Haunted houses—Fiction.
5. Michigan—Fiction.   I. Title.
PS3614.E585S65   2011
813'.6—dc22   2011020859

TO MY MOTHER,

Gloria,

MY BIGGEST FAN

Prologue

~ *I was twelve years old before the tooth fairy first visited me and left fifty* cents under my pillow. My father forbade our believing in angels, trolls, saints, spirits, ghosts and fairies of any kind. But the god who takes care of little kids smiled on me one evening at a slumber party at Jimmy VandenBerg's house and caused me to lose a tooth in a handful of Cracker Jack. Jimmy's mom kindly washed the tooth and wrapped it in gauze, and then explained that fairies know where everyone is at all times, and that it wasn't necessary to wait until I got home to put it under my pillow. I suspect she had been to PTA meetings where my father extolled the virtues of eliminating school celebrations of Halloween, and she likely concluded that a twelve-year-old coming home with a tooth and a wish wouldn't get a particularly enthusiastic reception from him.

I'm not sure if I believed there really was a tooth fairy, but I remember sliding my hand under the pillow the next morning, even before I opened my eyes.

I did, however, know for a fact that there was no such thing as a ghost.

The story you are about to read happened up in Michigan, where people are pragmatic and life can be pretty rugged, given the snow and cold and seasonal layoffs and endless gray skies we have to cope with every winter. It can make you feel like there's a camera on somewhere, and a director hoping to get enough footage of you having a miserable time so he can make a prizewinning documentary on surviving life in the far and dreary North. As for the rest of the seasons, they aren't much better. Just when things are starting to look up in spring, the blackflies arrive, leaving dime-sized welts and their telltale trickle of blood on any piece of skin that isn't covered. And you want to talk about slugs? Our neighbors catch them through the summer in shallow bowls of beer they anchor in the dirt around their vegetables. The biggest I ever saw was about six inches long and round as a nickel, mustard yellow with black spots and dead drunk. It could have had its own sci-fi series. We gave it to the chickens.

Snowmobiles figure in more deaths than cars in a lot of small towns up here. It's kids, mostly, going too fast, being too drunk, and ending up under the front wheels of a car or smashed into the base of a tree. I read once about a guy who was decapitated by a length of old barbed wire he hit going fifty mph through a frozen cow pasture. His headless torso twitched in the snow for two minutes.

My point is that people in our neck of the woods don't have the need or inclination to spin yarns. Our real lives furnish plenty of material.

This is the story of one old house and one middle-aged married couple.

Anna, my wife, called it a nightmare. But nightmares are dreams. This was as real as water. We tell this story together and alternate to give you a 360-degree perspective. That's necessary because, as you'll see, we lied to each other. Neither of us, yet, has the whole picture.

One

   Maple Hill had been situated on Lake Street in Carlston, Michigan, for 121 years by the time John and I first saw it. On that particular afternoon, silver and red Christmas garland wrapped the front pillars, and swags of plastic evergreen were anchored at each corner of the porch roof with red velveteen bows. On the porch itself, three white wicker rockers with red striped cushions were lined up side-by-side, and on each seat lay a pinecone wreath tied with red ribbons. The chairs were flanked by twin, life-sized grapevine deer covered in white lights. A six-foot cardboard cutout of Santa Claus stood just to the right of the front door. Inside, an electric candle glowed in each window, and we could see colored lights blinking dimly from somewhere behind them in most of the front rooms. Even the "For Sale" sign in the yard had a red bow on it.

It was mid-July.

"Well, at least it doesn't look abandoned," I told John. "Maybe the owner just likes Christmas."

We called a realtor and arranged to see it a few days later. And that's how we came to meet Margaret, the owner.

"It's my favorite season," she told us as she led us around the house. "I never take down the decorations completely. Sometimes I pack away a few things, but I always put up more. This house just asks to be stuffed with Christmas!"

3

John rolled his eyes for my benefit alone.

There was a decorated artificial tree in nearly every room, including the first-floor bath, and plug-in air fresheners made the whole place smell like cinnamon and baked apples. For as warm and bright as it was outside, it felt like the dark days of December inside. Margaret had hung heavy brocade drapes over most of the windows, and her furniture was big and broody, leaving little room to walk. Not the picture of grace under the best of circumstances, I bumped into a grapevine reindeer rearing precariously on two of its hoofs, which crashed into a side table and sent a bowl of potpourri sailing.

Margaret asked if we had kids as she led us up the stairway to the bedrooms on the second floor.

I told her no, but I was mostly distracted trying to navigate around a dozen or so fabric cats wearing red and green calico bonnets and occupying a significant part of each step. The banister was wrapped in garland, too, which left little room to grab hold, and I was trying to avoid another stumble. There was more. Brittle spruce cones hung by ribbons that were thumbtacked into the window ledge, and Christmas cards lay heaped in a silver bowl on the landing. I couldn't imagine how someone could walk up and down those stairs every day, carrying laundry or even just a coffee cup. I guess Margaret was used to it. Meanwhile, she was clearly disappointed by my answer about kids. With the big yard and all, she had hoped a family with lots of children would buy the place.

The upstairs hall was wide, which was a relief, and the rooms that opened on to it were in various stages of renovation. Maybe that's being generous. Some of the rooms looked like they hadn't been touched in years. Dusty garland draped each doorway, and wreaths made of some kind of artificial greenery hung by suction cups in most of the windows.

The closets were small and covered with curtains instead of doors. And the floors were so slanted that a fair game of marbles wouldn't have been possible.

I asked Margaret why there were no doors on the closets. She had just drawn aside a lace panel that didn't quite reach to the floor and did only a passable job of screening out the clutter of suits and men's pressed shirts behind it.

"I don't think this house had any closets when it was built," Margaret replied, leaning against her dresser. "And there sure weren't many when we moved in three years ago. We carved out a few, but none of them have standard-size openings, so we just hung curtains instead of trying to fit them with custom-made doors."

I remember squeezing John's hand. He smiled. I knew we would deal with the curtain issue later. Margaret suggested we finish with a tour of the basement, and I'll tell you, the thought of just trying to get there was daunting.

"You first," John offered. He sounded gallant, but it was really self-defense. Margaret led the way back down to the front hall stairs, through the living and dining rooms and into the kitchen to a five-foot-tall door in the back corner to the left of the sink.

It was tricky getting down the narrow basement stairs. John thinks they were added when the outdoor access was bricked shut sometime in the early 1900s. Fitted between an old waste pipe, two support beams and the foundation wall, it was a clever project for the tiny space.

"The steps are treacherous, but you'll get used to them," Margaret told us as she started down first.

I gripped the block wall and took a deep breath. The air was cool compared to the heat outside, and it had that characteristic musty old basement smell. Margaret didn't exaggerate the state of the steps. They were awful, but there were only eight of them. When I reached the bottom, I stood still for a few moments waiting for my eyes to adjust to the relative darkness. We were in a small, windowless room dominated by a giant and very old furnace that sat silent in the July heat, looking deceptively ready for the next cold spell. Margaret said it had been converted twice—once from coal to oil, then again to gas. John figured it would need to be replaced before winter set in.

Beyond the tiny furnace room was another room that was likely used to store coal at one time and who knows what else. The floor space measured only about twelve feet by twelve feet, and each side ended at a block wall about four feet high. From that block wall to the outside wall—a space of about five feet—it was all dirt, sloping from that short wall gradually upward toward the foundation. It was a typical Michigan crawl space, Margaret told us. The area left just enough room for someone to crawl around to fix wiring or plumbing or a loose board in the floor above. The dirt, having seen neither rain or snow nor any other elements for over a century, was bone dry, almost powdery.

In many places the dirt had been covered with old boards and doors to make a sort of deep shelf where seasonal things like canning jars and flower bulbs could be stored safely on top in the cool darkness. Margaret kept her unused Christmas decorations there. John said it might also be just about perfect for storing wine.

There was a relatively new water heater, two old worktables and not much more, except for a tangle of new and old water pipes and the remnants of ancient wiring that hadn't been removed when the electrical service was upgraded. We headed back up the stairs into the kitchen.

I couldn't resist. "Is it haunted?" I asked, trying to sound casual. With more than one hundred years' worth of families having walked its halls, I figured somebody interesting must have stuck around.

"No," Margaret replied, looking slightly off-put by my question. "There's nothing like that going on here."

John asked why they were moving. Margaret told us that her husband had been transferred. His law firm had decided to open an office in Cleveland, and they wanted him to head it up. It was one of those offers that are too good to pass up, but they were real sad to leave the house. She said they thought they would otherwise have lived there forever. Then she switched the subject and offered us iced tea.

~ *Anna said later that she couldn't imagine living "forever" in a house that* was so dark and cluttered and perennially blinking with Christmas lights. But Margaret's answer did explain why she and her husband had gone to the trouble and expense of shoring up the foundation and replacing several crumbling plaster walls with drywall. Yet, in spite of what they had already accomplished, the place needed a ton of work. Many walls in the bedrooms upstairs were covered with old wallpaper that would have to be removed before painting. It did occur to me, however, that the paper might be the only thing keeping the walls from cracking. The bathrooms needed to be gutted and rebuilt, and the kitchen felt like a cave, with brown cabinets, brown paneling and brown vinyl flooring. I assumed the electrical service, even though "updated," was minimal, and Anna has already told you about the furnace. As I added up costs in my head, I estimated replacement of that beast alone at somewhere around $5,000.

And there was something else that wasn't really a problem in the grand scheme of renovating the house, but was certainly unattractive. The yard was pocked with what looked like twenty or thirty abandoned flower beds—smallish plots of lawn that had been dug up rather randomly around the one-acre lot, seemingly with good intentions, then given over to weeds. I thought, at first, they were the work of a dog with too much time on his hands. But Margaret didn't have a dog. And she apparently didn't have a green thumb, either. There wasn't a healthy-looking flower or vegetable plant anywhere on the grounds. Not a petunia or rosebush to be found. No herbs or tomatoes, not even an old bed of peonies or a leggy lilac bush. Nothing but those tufts of turned-over ground, some rugged old spruce that probably predated the house, and a row of fine, ancient maples along the north property line for which the place was named. Getting this place in shape, both inside and out, would be a huge expensive project.

Anna started gushing before we were barely out of the driveway. It was clear that she loved it.

"Did you catch her reaction when I asked about ghosts?" she asked me. She was digging through her purse to find the directions to the restaurant where we were meeting the realtor so we could talk.

"She thought you were nuts," I told Anna. She read off the directions, and I followed. It wasn't far.

Anna said she should have anticipated Margaret's reaction just by the religious pictures all over the house and the framed Bible passages in the kitchen. But she was hoping for some stories. Not that Margaret would have told her the truth anyway. I imagine that owners who want to sell keep the details of unexplained phenomena to themselves.

I turned into a parking spot and shut off the car. In the two minutes it took us to go from the house to the diner, Anna had already sketched the first floor and found places to put our piano, the pie safe, and the cranberry love seat that had been her grandmother's. I put my arms around her and suggested that she not get emotionally involved with the house, yet. And I started to enumerate the reasons why. But I gave up when I saw the expression on her face. I had seen it before. She was smiling and pretending to listen. I knew in her mind it was a done deal.

"Too late?" I asked.

"Yep, I think so," Anna said, grabbing her papers, and she was out of the car in a second.

Jayne Tolbert was our realtor. She's gorgeous and funny, and we both liked her a lot. She and Anna were whispering conspiratorially by the time I came out of the bathroom and headed to their table. Anna suggested that maybe Margaret would find our offer more acceptable if we promised to keep all that garland up for sixty days after closing. That made Jayne laugh. For three years, she had driven past the house nearly every evening on her way home from work. She told us the decorations were at one time a topic of considerable talk in town, but the novelty had worn off, and now the place was just something that made people shake their heads. Jayne had figured it would take an outsider to get past the weirdness of it. And Anna certainly seemed to have gotten past it.

Jayne apologized at least three times for having turned us loose alone with Margaret. She had an unexpected financing problem at a closing just before our appointment to tour the house, and hadn't been able to take us through herself. She didn't like to leave potential buyers in the hands of the owners because she thought sometimes they were less than forthright about their home's condition. But in this case, she felt that underneath all the lights and tinsel, we would find a pretty solid house.

I can't help but have questions about that day, the timing of our finding the house, Jayne's meeting that kept her from joining us. I've wondered how different things might be if we had waited until the next day to tour the house, or the next week, when she could have gone through it with us. Maybe someone else would have seen it first and put in an offer, and we would have found another place.

"Consider yourselves lucky if she leaves that garland up," Jayne offered. "There has to be two hundred dollars' worth across the porch roofs and up those pillars."

"Anna's always wanted an old house," I told her. I remember looking at my sweet wife of less than six months and shaking my head. I reached for the sketch in her lap and held it up to show Jayne. "She has places for the furniture already!"

  It was true, this dream of mine to have a big old place. I told John about it early on in our courtship in case he was inclined to chrome and plastic. I wanted flower and vegetable gardens, too. Years of apartment living had confined my passion for gardening to window boxes and patio tomatoes. This house would give me nearly an acre to play with. And

8

John could have a dog. But first things first. John had questions. He turned to me and asked if I could live in a house without closet doors.

My face got hot, and I put my hands over my eyes. I knew this was coming. One night a couple years earlier when we were dating, I stopped John mid-kiss and asked if he would please close the bedroom closet door. He thought it was an odd request in the midst of some world-class foreplay, but he got up and pushed the door lightly, never taking his eyes off me. So he didn't notice that the door didn't quite close. I asked him to try again. He got a bit exasperated and asked if he was falling in love with a neat freak. But he did get up once more, and this time he hit the door with his hip, slamming it tight.

I told him that things live in closets.

Sitting there in front of Jayne, he was grinning from ear to ear, remembering that conversation.

I said I would just have to get used to it, and John immediately realized that kind of stuff really does unhinge me. He softened and took my hand and told me he would look for some doors that could be cut down to fit. And then he laughed and reminded me that we didn't even own the place yet.

An hour later, we held a copy of our offer, which Jayne would hand-carry to Margaret, and we headed back to our apartment.

‿ *It was late afternoon already, and warm. Anna and I drove the old road,* past the city beach and the little bar that served fried perch. A few miles later, I wheeled into the parking lot of the state park and asked Anna if she wanted to go for a walk.

She shouted yes and bolted out of the car, yelling over her shoulder, "I'll race you!" Halfway to the shore, she kicked off her shoes without slowing down.

After three years of dating and six months of marriage, I still loved just looking at Anna. So I sat there for a minute thinking how good my life was. Then I opened my door and pulled off my shoes and socks and tucked them behind the front seat. I took out a small cooler, a paper bag and a towel from the trunk and headed for the water. I remember feeling the sand, so warm on the soles of my feet. Anna and I love living near these incredible beaches.

Anna was already up to her knees in Lake Michigan. It had been unseasonably hot and the water was over seventy degrees. She waved and yelled to me, but the offshore wind blew her words away. I held up the cooler for her to see, then spread the towel and sat and watched her play.

"The water's wonderful," she said, walking toward me a few minutes later. The hems of her shorts were wet, and she was out of breath. Then she kneeled down next to me and held her hands out and asked, "What's all this?"

I said I thought she might get thirsty. I took a bottle of champagne, two very cold glasses and a dozen strawberries from the cooler. Cheese and crackers were in the bag. She was suddenly all over me, in what started as a hug and ended with both of us on our backs in the sand.

Early in our relationship, I surprised Anna by meeting her plane, unannounced, when she returned from a long weekend with friends in Maine. Until then, we had barely kissed during the months we had been casually seeing each other, but she had called me from a pay phone near the harbor bait shop every night she was away. She told me about the big snowstorm that hit the first day and the sound of the waves on the rocks and the brightness of the stars. She told me she thought we were falling in love. Still, I guess seeing me at her gate was a big surprise. I lived three hours away at the time, and I had to be at work the next morning by nine A.M. Then I gave her a second surprise, a feast of cheese and champagne I had stashed in a cooler in the back seat.

I stayed with her that night and left before dawn to make the 150-mile drive to work, and we've been having romantic picnics ever since. Anna says when we pass on, she wants our friends and family to hold a picnic instead of a funeral.

Margaret accepted our offer. I think she liked us, despite our being childless. She and her husband said they had faith that the sale would go through, and they began packing for Cleveland immediately. Two weeks later they dropped by our apartment. Their car was filled to the roof with the most fragile of their Christmas ornaments, and they handed us their keys. In mid-September, after annoying delays waiting for surveys and inspection reports, the house was ours. The night we closed the deal, Anna and I ate our first dinner at Maple Hill—baked sweet potatoes and half a pound of Brie, plus a bottle of the best white wine we could find at the Gas'n'Go. We made love in the parlor on the bare oak floor, sat on the front porch and watched the moon rise, then laid out sleeping bags and pillows retrieved from our storage locker and slept on the carpeted floor in the empty master bedroom.

ໄ *Carlston is a pretty town, a bit hilly, with three blocks of turn-of-the-* century homes, a few old brick edifices still standing in the downtown and a postcard-worthy spread of rolling farmland and maples that stretch west to Lake Michigan. Four-mile-long Crab Lake borders the town's eastern edge, then funnels into a natural channel that drains into Lake Michigan. The area was first platted as Lumbertown until state officials discovered that seven new logging towns, springing up as fast as the forests around them were coming down, wanted the same descriptive name. The village fathers held a quick meeting one night and decided instead to honor Thomas Carl, who had built the first lumber mill on Crab Lake and had once owned most of the land on which the town was growing. So Carlston was born. Thomas was voted mayor in the next election, was reelected a couple times after that, then retired graciously to a cabin on several acres he had cleared in his youth. His son Sam, who took over the lumber business, lived long enough to see the boom and bust of Carlston, the clear-cutting of nearly all the state's marketable pine, and the inevitable closing of all ten lumber mills around Crab Lake when the forests were gone. He liked to take the train to Chicago every year around Christmas and walk through downtown, remembering that his father's pine had helped rebuild the city after its great fire.

Sam had one of the first automobiles to rattle up Main Street. He marveled at the telephone and the airplane, and while he missed the bustle of his early milling days, he thought the closing of six of the town's eight taverns and two houses of ill repute was a good thing. He lived comfortably into his eighty-third year and was buried in the family plot, next to Sarah Katharine, his wife of forty-two years.

All that remains of the Ottawa Indians who once lived peacefully along the shores of Crab Lake is a small burial ground at the foot of Dock Street, a block from Maple Hill. An old house encroaches on one side of it, and the north corner was paved over in the '30s. Now the area is designated with a small wooden marker as a historic site. There are no written records listing those who were laid to rest there. The graves were never marked, and the oldest known surviving descendant who once might have had ancestral knowledge of the site lives twenty-three miles and three-quarters of a lifetime away, in a nursing home. The true boundaries of the once-sacred ground are known only to those who lie within them.

I learned most of this from a small hand-printed, hand-bound book that I found in the museum—an ambitious history project written sixty years ago by a local high school student. By the time John and I arrived on the scene, Carlston was a quiet town with few remnants of its raucous heyday. Its residents now are a peaceful mix of locals and newcomers—the first being those who have been around long enough to recall ten-cent sodas at Timm's Ice Cream Parlor and the names of the two draft horses that pulled Santa in the Christmas parade on Main Street during World War II. "Newcomers" covers just about everyone else, with the exception of the few folks who left Carlston to go to college and returned to make a living. The townspeople are friendly and politely curious. Neighbors brought cookies and flowers from their gardens when they saw our rented U-Haul parked in the driveway. They commiserated with us about the hassles of moving, and they gave us the names of reliable electricians and plumbers. Two weeks after we moved in, John made plans to fly to San Francisco.

In the years since college, John has managed to advance his youthful enthusiasm for wine into a profitable business, selling supplies and advice to wine masters all over the country. He is sharp and smart and fun. Winemakers like his sense of humor and the way he understands the quirky nature of grapes. But more than that, John listens carefully when they talk about the challenges they face with each new season and vintage. He has an uncanny ability to diagnose trouble and usually can find solutions. Most Monday mornings he boards a plane and heads to a winery, somewhere between the Atlantic and the Pacific. John loves his work . . .

↪ . . . *except that it took me away from Anna every week.*

She was sitting on our bed on a Sunday night, watching me pack. It was my first business trip since we moved in. I figured she would be a little lonely while I was gone, but I wasn't prepared for her sudden and quiet confession.

"Guess I better figure out how I'm going to sleep in this old house alone and not be afraid."

I stopped folding my shirts and turned to look at her, expecting to see a teasing smile. There was none.

"You're kidding, aren't you?"

"About being afraid or getting over it?"

I asked her why we bought an old house if she was going to be afraid. She said she would be fine. I remember her exact words.

"I'll get over it."

"What are you afraid of?" I asked. "You don't have to be worried about intruders. We have good locks on the doors. And anyway, break-ins don't seem to happen much in this town."

"No, they don't," Anna began. "But that's not what scares me. It's the spooky stuff . . . the stuff you can't lock out . . . little things like the faces and the voices of the past . . ."

I put my arms around her and kissed her forehead, trying not to laugh. She was being so serious. "Oh, that. I'm sorry, I didn't know this would be difficult for you." It was all I could think to say.

She said, again, that she would be fine. And she reminded me that she was the one who pushed to get this house. She told me how she had gone into the basement the day before when I was at the store, just so she could poke around and get used to things a bit.

"It's a good house, John. It feels comfortable. I wasn't scared at all. I looked around to see if anybody left us any treasures, and I hugged the old support beams and patted the furnace and asked it to please make it through the winter."

I could see Anna doing that. She makes friends with strangers on first meeting like they've known each other forever, so it didn't surprise me that she would do the same with the beams and the furnace.

"You'll be OK," I said. It was a weak response, but truthfully, I was preoccupied with getting ready for my trip. In just two weeks, I had grown very fond of being in our new home with Anna, and though I loved my job, leaving Anna behind and facing four nights in a hotel didn't hold much appeal at that point. I kissed her again, then went back to packing. About ten minutes later, I zipped up the suitcase and put it in the hall. Anna had climbed in bed and was under the covers, writing in the journal I bought her as a welcome-home present. I walked downstairs to the kitchen and poured glasses of juice for both of us, then noticed that the basement door was ajar. I pulled it shut and laughed to myself. Anna would be pleased with me, I thought. Things probably lived in basements, too.

❧ *My first night alone was uneventful. John called at nine o'clock to say good* night and we talked for a few minutes as we did every night we were apart.

He asked if I was afraid. I said no. A half truth.

13

"I miss you," he said. "Four days and I'll be home again. I'll call you tomorrow."

I watched television until ten o'clock. I had left on two lights in the living room, the light in the foyer and—for good measure—a light in the kitchen. Then I walked upstairs sideways so I could look both up the stairs and down. Have you ever done that? When I watch scary old movies, I always wonder why the heroine, bravely climbing the stairs to investigate a noise, only looks ahead of her and doesn't think to look back down the stairs to see what evil might be following her. And God only knows why those clueless women never turn on any lights. I brushed my teeth quietly so I would hear any odd sounds, put on a flannel nightgown and a pair of John's sweatpants, and climbed under the covers. I watched more TV for about an hour, then picked up a paperback and read till midnight, when the book jerked in my hands and I realized, gratefully, that I was falling asleep.

Perfect, I thought. No chance that I'll lie here half the night with my eyes open. I put the book on top of the blanket on John's side of the bed, turned out the light on my nightstand, turned it on again and closed my eyes. I'm sure I was asleep in less than a minute. The night light in the bathroom burned brightly. Had I awakened early, I would most likely have seen it dim briefly, as it always did, when the furnace kicked on sometime in the chilly hours just before dawn.

~ *October passed quickly, and the maples turned a glowing yellow-red,* reaching peak just before Halloween. Anna got a part-time job writing special features for our little weekly newspaper. She had proposed to the editor that she highlight unusual accomplishments and hobbies of various townspeople—the inventor who held patents for mechanical parts used in the aeronautics industry, the farmer who raised angora goats and sold hand-spun yarn to costume designers in Hollywood, the soprano who had starred in several off-Broadway musicals before she retired to the lake. It was easy writing, and she was good at it. She met lots of people in town as she went in search of stories, and the work distracted her from thoughts of otherworld visitors roaming our house.

Margaret had advised us to plan for about sixty trick-or-treaters, so Anna bought bags of chocolate peanut butter cups and filled a basket in the front hall. She also stocked up on red licorice for me, and I surprised her by catching an early flight home from Albany so I could arrive in time to help with the handouts.

The porch was decorated with pumpkin lights, bales of straw and bundles of cornstalks. Anna had carved two pumpkins earlier in the week, too. Their lids were sooty and shrinking from the candles she had burned in them every night, and through their toothy smiles you could see puddles of melted wax in assorted colors.

The afternoon was unseasonably warm, and it rolled into an almost balmy evening, so we parked ourselves in rocking chairs on the porch with a bottle of wine and bread sticks between us, and we picnicked between trick-or-treaters.

This was the first time I noticed that Anna had a nasty cough. I asked when she got it, as a little group of goblins and princesses raced off the porch and hurried on to the next house.

The sidewalk looked momentarily clear, so she settled back and pulled a shawl around her shoulders.

"It just came on yesterday," she replied, picking through the candy and counting to see if we had enough left. "It's not a big deal."

I leaned across the arm of my chair and kissed her cheek, though I was really trying to see if she felt feverish. She looked tired. She had been so tan in August and was now quite pale.

"Why don't you go inside and let me finish up out here," I offered. It was nearly eight o'clock anyway and the city's designated trick-or-treat hours were about over.

She said she was fine.

"We have enough candy for about forty more kids," Anna continued. "Guess I got carried away, but I couldn't stand the thought of running out. Margaret told me she ran out once and started handing out dimes and nickels, and the kids loved it. Then she realized that she was seeing some of the same kids come around a second time, so she switched to pennies!"

"Did that put an end to the second-timers?"

"Yeah. The little kids loved the pennies, and the older kids didn't come back. You know, I think some of the kids we had tonight were so old they probably would have preferred a glass of our wine to the candy!"

Something suddenly caught our attention on the sidewalk. Walking toward the porch, apparently alone, was a tiny angel, dressed head to toe in pink, with starched wings and a silver halo attached to a headband. We were both speechless. She couldn't have been more than three. She climbed the stairs slowly and held out her bag for treats.

"Well, hello, little one," Anna greeted her and put a handful of candy in her bag. The girl whispered a thank you. She was the cutest thing, really. Then she turned and reached out an arm as though looking for a hand to help her back down the porch steps.

Suddenly this adult voice yelled "Happy Halloween!" from the dark, and Anna and I about fell out of our chairs. Anna actually shrieked. We had been so captivated by the sight of the child we hadn't even seen her mother standing off to the side in the shadows. She moved into the light of the porch. And that was how we met Grace Booth.

She apologized heartily for startling us and reached out to steady the angel. Then she shook our hands with a grip like a carpenter's and welcomed us to the neighborhood. We introduced ourselves. Anna was laughing by then and said Grace was the best scare we'd had all night.

꿩 *Turns out that Grace and her husband, Ed, had come to an open house at* our home earlier in the summer, before we bought it. They weren't particularly interested in buying Maple Hill but were real curious about what it looked like inside. They both grew up around Carlston and had never been in the house before. They wondered who had finally bought it.

Well, you're looking at them, I told her, and I asked if the child was her daughter.

"This is my angel, Bethany," Grace told us. She picked the little girl up. "It's her first Halloween. She's only two and a half, but she really wanted to do this, so I thought a few houses might be fun for her. We just live around the corner."

Bethany smiled and put her head on Grace's shoulder. She was a beauty. We invited Grace to come back sometime when she could stay for coffee. I told her I wanted to write the history of the house and would love to hear about any memories that she or her husband had of it.

Grace thanked us as she headed down the walk. "I'll stop by in the daylight when I don't have a thirty-pound angel on my shoulder," she said. Then she gave me the best news of all. She worked at the library and invited me to come and look through the history files to see if we could find some background on the house. It was a great ending to our first Halloween at Maple Hill.

~ *"John, come and see what I found!"*

I heard this often from Anna. She was skilled at digging up information about the town and its old residents and our house, and she almost always had something new to show me when I came home. On that particular morning, Anna had walked up the street to the county maritime museum and was studying the displays for clues and stories about the families who had lived here, and that's when she met Kathy Clark. Kathy is passionate about local history and has voluntarily run the museum for nearly a decade. She is a tireless gatherer of artifacts and mementos, and among her treasures are three file cabinets of old photos and negatives and postcards of the area. Together, she and Anna had spent most of that morning sorting through each drawer until, no surprise to Kathy, they found a small envelope marked "Maple Hill." Anna ran most of the way home to show me her latest treasures.

❧ *There was a local photographer who worked here in town for decades, until* 1930, when he retired and moved to Chicago to be closer to his daughters. He took tons of shots all around this side of the state, and he also collected other people's photos. Then he cataloged everything, which was a remarkable accomplishment, and donated it all to the city before he left town. The city gave the collection to the museum when it opened ten years ago. And that is how Kathy and I came to find the photos of the James family, who lived in our house until 1919.

I emptied the contents of the envelope—seven fading photographs—onto the dining room table. Three were small, formal studio portraits. One showed a solemn man and a woman with dark, sad eyes. She is sitting, he is standing behind her. The woman is holding an infant in a long christening gown. A little boy stands to her right. The second was of the husband and wife without the children, and the third was of the baby alone, lying in a crib, dressed in a long gown and a light-colored sweater fastened in the front with three pearl buttons. The baby is looking at the camera.

Three of the other photos showed the house and grounds. The big

17

front porch had two rocking chairs on it and was surrounded by blooming spirea. The maple trees in the front yard were no bigger around than a person's wrist. And there were two photos of gardens lush with bushes and flowers that appeared to thrive in the sandy soil.

The last photo was taken much later than the others. It showed a young man in uniform. "Andre James" was written on the back in pencil.

Kathy said we could keep them for a few days. In fact, she encouraged me to take them to a photo shop and have copy prints made.

〜 *Anna held the photo of the woman and children up to her face and tried* to replicate their dour expressions. "Any resemblance?"

"I have never seen you look that unhappy," I told her. "Life must have been terribly hard for them. Can you imagine the winters here without a forced-air furnace?"

"And dinner, clucking in the backyard?" Anna laughed until she started to cough.

I asked if she had called the doctor yet. She said she had and that she had picked up a prescription for something.

"Did you take any?" I asked her. "You know, it's not enough just to pick it up. You've got to put it in a spoon and actually swallow it ..." I know she dislikes conventional medications of all sorts and is more inclined to reach for an old herbal book and make a concoction out of things like eye of newt and tail of toad.

"GET OUT OF MY HOUSE!"

I stood in the living room, arms outstretched, and yelled at the walls. "Get out of my house! This is MY house. We live here, now. It's not your house anymore. LEAVE! GET OUT ... GET OUT!"

John came home Friday from St. Louis.

"Who would have thought anybody could make good wine in Missouri?" he mused in the car when I picked him up at the airport. "But it's not bad, really. They're shipping a case to our house this week so you can try it, too. They don't export much outside the state. I think they're hoping we'll like it a lot and tell all our wine-drinking friends and they'll find themselves with a profitable market in the North."

"Pretty big expectations to put on two people who live in a town of less than three thousand," I laughed. "With all the wine we have downstairs, maybe we should just open a shop. You know, like the big beer stores, we could advertise 275 varieties of wine . . ."

". . . and no more than ten bottles of any one type!" John added.

"And don't forget twenty-three styles of personalized corkscrews, and several dozen towels with winery monograms. What does it matter if they've never heard of Bruised Apple Cellars or Pungent Rock? Maybe we could soak off all the labels so everybody would get potluck. That would certainly be a new concept in wine buying!"

One of the side benefits of John's work was the supply of wine and glasses and wine-cellar accessories that vintners sent home with him after business trips. Sometimes they had bottles of champagne delivered at the holidays or new releases for us to try. Most of the wines we received were quite good—wine makers seldom sent us less than their best. Once, John received a jeroboam of merlot for his birthday from Crooked Peak, a tiny winery in Washington State. They had asked his advice on solving the problem of an unpleasant burnt-sugar aftertaste in their reds, and they were winning international medals eighteen months after his diagnosis. Meanwhile, after pondering what to do with such an awesome gift, we called a dozen friends, bought six pounds of portobello mushroom caps, a brick of cheddar and a couple bags of buns; several pounds of potato salad, coleslaw and baked beans; plus two half gallons of Mackinac Island Fudge ice cream, and had a fabulous cookout. In case you didn't know, merlot and Mackinac Island Fudge ice cream were made for each other.

John had been right about the basement being good for wine storage. He had taken one section of the crawl space and stacked wooden wine crates seven wide and four high. With the addition of a few shims here and there, the vertical fit was tight, and the top crates were wedged against the ceiling joists. About half the spaces in the crates were filled with generous client offerings.

It was March, and the driveway was muddy from persistent rains. John grabbed his bags and followed me into the house. I remember I was wearing a gray skirt that gathered at my waist and swept close enough to the ground to get wet and spattered. My blouse was gray, too, and my long hair was pulled back into a bun.

I had made soup for supper, and started to set the table. John picked up some drawings from the counter and turned them around several times, trying to make sense of them. They were my garden plans.

He asked how the house felt to me, now that the ground was thawing and I would soon be able to start planting.

I told him it was OK.

I look back at that evening occasionally and try to remember what I was really thinking. I had begun to dress like a widow, but didn't seem to notice, and I no longer made the wonderful roasted vegetables and salads that John loved. Instead, I made soup nearly every day and spent hours baking bread. I brought our food to the table and wondered if John felt the same urge as I to go out into the damp cold and dig some new garden beds.

~ *Anna had chilled a bottle of wine—Chateau Nevermore we called it. It* was our nickname for a winery in western Minnesota that bottled everything in black glass. The label had a stylized drawing of a tree in winter and a raven landing on one of the branches. In spite of having a short growing season and desperately cold winters, the winery put out a good product. I had ordered a case of their barrel-select Chardonnay after we drank the gift case that showed up around Thanksgiving. I told Anna I hope I never slip and call it Nevermore in front of the owners.

Anna brought fresh-baked bread to the table. It smelled great, and when I asked what it was she told me she had made it up. Flour, water, salt, oil, yeast. She said it seemed pretty simple. It was outstanding.

Maybe if the bread hadn't been so good, I would have noticed the odd clothes sooner.

"You asked how I feel about the house," Anna said. "Well, you know, nothing unusual happens, like I don't find lights on that I already turned off, or things out of place." Then she started to laugh as she looked around at the stacks of old magazines and catalogs and unpacked boxes and the general chaos of our renovation-in-progress. I read her mind. "As if we could tell if anything was out of place," I said.

"Yeah, but it's not that. And I don't see bodies floating above the floor in long white dresses or hear babies crying. It's just that sometimes I feel like I'm being shadowed. Or watched. It's creepy. And this week I read about how sometimes spirits need to know who's boss, so I stood in the living room and yelled at them and told them to go away. I told them this is our house now."

"Did they answer?" Oh, Lord, I should have taken this seriously, but I was too amused. Anna, of course, ignored my question.

"I don't know if there's anything to any of this, but I felt better. I mean, I didn't feel so bugged. Physically, I still feel like hell because this cold is hanging on."

I suggested that she rest over the weekend. I told her I would take care of the house and the laundry and stuff so she could stay in bed. Two days of doing nothing might go a long way to helping her kick whatever was ailing her.

Anna looked relieved, which startled me. I hadn't realized she was still feeling so bad. She had battled a cold and the flu for much of the winter, but she seldom complained and mostly brushed aside my questions about her health. In all the time I had known her, she seemed blessed with a tough constitution. She hadn't done much more than sneeze that I could remember, and she'd never broken a bone or sprained a limb in her life.

"Maybe I'll take you up on your offer," she said flatly. She said she was very tired. Then she offered me more soup. I told her I'd get it. She hadn't finished her own, yet. I watched as she got into bed that night and realized she was thinner.

Spring was slow in coming and brief that year. Deep into April the air still held a frigid chill, and a freak snowstorm in early May kept the buds tight on flowering trees until well past their usual time to open. When at last the weather turned warm, everything bloomed at once for ten glorious days. Then the petals fell into a thick carpet overnight during a dazzling thunderstorm, and it was summer.

"Wait till you hear this," Anna yelled. She came running up the front walk and parked herself in the rocker next to me. It was nearly noon on a bright Saturday just before Memorial Day, and I was catching up on my reading. When we moved to Carlston, Anna got me a subscription to the Sunday *New York Times*, which I loved, and I was slowly wading through it, putting off reading the half-dozen trade journals that were waiting for me as well. Anna had been at the library since it opened at nine o'clock, and her hand was waving a legal pad full of notes.

"You know how I've been trying to track down the history of this house?" I must have nodded, but I really wasn't listening, and I never looked up. She put her arms around me to get my attention.

"Listen, really, this is incredible. Please." I remember folding the newspaper and looking at her. Anna could get pretty dramatic and fixated on whatever she was doing, and I had learned not to jump whenever she was excited about something. Lately, she was obsessed about finding out all she could on the house and the people who had lived there before us. I asked about her cough, though I know I was distracted by an article I was reading about a new wine grape being introduced in Upstate New York.

"OK. Listen. I have been getting the most incredible stories about the people who lived in this house. You remember those photos I got from the maritime museum?"

"The James family?"

"Yes. Oh, John, it's so sad." And out poured the story.

Their names were Martin and Jeanette. Jeanette was an orphan from Canada. Her mother, Ophelia, had come to Canada from France when she was about fourteen. She had fallen in love with a local Indian and married him while she was still quite young. Jeanette was their only child. They settled in Quebec, and then Jeanette's father was killed trying to break a horse, and her mother died in childbirth about two months later. Jeanette went to live with nuns.

Martin was a salesman who traveled all over the Upper Midwest and Canada. He met Jeanette, and they fell in love. That much had been documented.

Martin was the only surviving child of Edna and Abel James, who were still living in Carlston at that time. Jeanette didn't have any reason to stay in Quebec—no family there and few friends outside the convent, so they married and settled down in a small cabin near Crab Lake. A few years later, when Martin's business began to prosper, they bought Maple Hill and intended to have a long and happy life there.

"Poor thing," Anna concluded. "Can you imagine a sweet French Canadian Indian girl ending up in a backwater town like turn-of-the-century Carlston?"

I had put down my paper to listen to Anna's story. She was wearing the long gray skirt again, and a white blouse with short sleeves and a lace collar. Her hair was pulled into a bun.

"Are you hungry?" Anna asked. "Let's make some lunch, and I'll finish the story." She headed into the kitchen without an answer.

I had arrived home on a late flight the night before, made even later because the airport was fogged in for a couple hours. When I got to the foot of the stairs, I was too tired to carry up my bags, so I just dropped them there, and stepped around them again in the morning when I came down for coffee.

I started to apologize to no one in particular and decided to take the suitcase and briefcase upstairs before lunch, when I had the odd feeling that something was amiss. I looked around the living room for the first time since I'd left home on Monday and saw immediately what it was. In my absence, Anna had taken down the pictures of us and our families that had hung next to our corner cabinet and replaced them with copies of the photos she had found at the museum. They were blown up considerably larger than their original size and were matted in old frames that Anna had bought at a yard sale several years earlier.

❧ John asked me why I thought the story was sad. I didn't understand his question.

"The sad part," he repeated. "You said this was a sad story, but so far it sounds like the guy scored a great French wife who was probably a real good cook and who thought Carlston was pretty camp. And I bet she had big fun writing to her girlfriends back in Quebec regaling them with stories of life in the States."

Well, the truth is, her life turned ugly real fast. It was easy to read between the lines. The town didn't much like Jeanette. She was so different from them, being part French and part Indian. She had jet black hair and pale skin. She's so beautiful in the photos. And she didn't speak much English when she first got here.

"I imagine it was a bad case of prejudice," I said. "Carlston in 1915 probably wasn't a stellar example of racial tolerance and brotherly love."

You can't imagine it.

"You can't imagine it," I said.

I told John how they did OK for a few years, but then Martin went on a long business trip in the spring of 1919 that took him across the Straits of Mackinac and up into Canada. He came down with the Spanish influenza there. You may remember that people were dying from it in huge numbers. Casket makers were working day and night to keep up with the demand. Martin died less than a week after he took ill.

People were so freaked by the sickness and the speed with which it spread that they wouldn't even return his body to Michigan. They buried him in Canada, in a small country cemetery, alongside several other travelers who had suffered the same fate.

~ Jeanette must have been devastated. But the story got worse. I was in-trigued now.

"Remember the photo of the little baby in the sweater?" Anna asked me.

How could I forget. I had just seen the enlargement hanging on my living room wall.

"She got sick, too, while Martin was in Canada. And then she dis-appeared, and her mother said she was kidnapped."

"That seems pretty far-fetched, Anna. Why on earth would some-one kidnap a sick child?"

While Anna was telling this story, she had heated a pot of soup and filled a bowl for each of us. It was good, as always, and I was halfway through mine before I realized she was talking so much that she had barely touched hers. She must have felt a coughing spasm come on then because she suddenly pushed herself back from the table and slapped a napkin over her mouth.

The coughing washed over her with the force of a hurricane hitting the Everglades. In seconds Anna was braced against the chair, hacking uncontrollably. I jumped up and put my arms around her, trying to still her violent shaking. The coughing went on for nearly a minute. It was intense and frightening. Then she broke into a sweat and began gasp-ing to catch her breath. I rubbed one hand up and down Anna's back, realizing I was absolutely powerless to help her. Slowly, unbearably slowly, she finally began to ease into a rhythmic, raspy panting and leaned against me, exhausted. It was only then that I noticed I had hit the end of my soup spoon in the commotion, causing it to pole-vault out of the bowl and leave a trail of minestrone on everything it hit be-fore it reached the floor. What a mess.

I told Anna I was going to put her to bed. I know I sounded sterner than I meant to, but I was shocked by the fierce attack. Anna's blond bangs were damp and stuck to her forehead. Her face was flushed and hot, and her eyes looked bright like she had a fever.

She said she wanted to finish telling me the story, but I told her it could wait.

It can't wait.

"It can't wait," she pleaded with me.

I took her arm to help her up—God, she was so weak. I was worried

24

that she hadn't eaten anything and asked if she wanted me to bring some soup up to bed for her. She told me it could wait.

You might not think my next move was the most ethical, but I was scared, and I didn't know what else to do. While Anna slept, I called her doctor and asked why she wasn't getting any better. It was the hardest phone call I ever made. Amazingly, in this small town, physicians list their home phone numbers in the local phone book.

"It seems that she has contracted some kind of virus that's settled in her lungs and chest," Dr. Lind told me. "These things can be hard to get rid of. The best we can do at this point is treat the symptoms and wait."

I asked about trying antibiotics.

"Not for a virus. They won't touch it. Other than the symptoms we're tracking, how does she seem?"

In fact, Anna's spirits were pretty high. When she wasn't coughing, she seemed to do OK. I was listening with one ear to the upstairs in case Anna got up, but the house was quiet.

Dr. Lind must have caught the hesitation in my voice. She had been seeing Anna since the first of the year for her respiratory problems, but had never met or spoken to me. She told me later that she wondered at the time what provoked me to call her at home on Saturday afternoon for something that didn't seem to be an emergency.

"What's the problem, John?"

How could I tell her about the odd clothes and pinned-up hair. And now the photos. It suddenly seemed a thin set of circumstances. I lowered my voice, mindful that Anna might wake up and come downstairs, and I said simply, "I'm a little puzzled . . ."

"Why?"

"Well, it's just a bunch of little things." I told her. I could feel my face getting hot. Was I nuts? Was I just being critical, or was something dreadfully wrong? I asked if I could come to Dr. Lind's office and talk to her.

"John, I can't talk about my patients when they're not present, unless it's to consult with other physicians. Can you and Anna come in together?"

I felt foolish and told her I would think about it. She said that after Anna's last bout of coughing, she wanted to have her come back in anyway so she could listen to her lungs and get another X-ray.

"Why don't you suggest that she make an appointment and ask her if you can come, too," the doctor offered. "I'll explain that there are some things you want to discuss, and if she's comfortable, we can go ahead and talk together."

❧ *John handed me a glass of juice and sat on the edge of the bed. That much I* remember. I had been sleeping for six hours. It was getting on toward dusk, and a warm front that had pushed through in the afternoon promised a brilliant sunset. It was so nice to have John home. I missed him terribly during the week, to the point that I had started fighting a battle with depression. Sometimes, for no apparent reason, I began to spiral down into the saddest state, feeling as though I had suffered great loss in my life and had little to live for. I thought back to my parents' death in a terrible car crash when I was young. My grandparents had taken me in immediately and loved me so completely that I had been spared the dark sense of loneliness that can invade and hold a child captive for decades. But I wondered if the pain had only been delayed until now. And why now? My life with John was so good. I was forty-one years old, a year younger than John, and happily married. Incredibly, it was a first marriage for both of us. A year earlier, before we were married, John and I decided we were past the point of having children, and that was fine with me. Was it possible that decision had triggered unresolved grief over my parents? Was the past tripping in thirty-two years later?

If you've ever been in love, deeply in love with someone, you probably know the fear of wondering if your feelings of sadness could be a premonition of tragedy, rather than a reaction to old events. I worried about that, too. Was something awful about to happen to John? Was his plane going to fall out of the sky? Would he suddenly confess to having a lover in California? Would a heart attack take him from me? I chewed on those—and a whole stack of other worries—for a while, then decided that it was probably nothing more that the fact that I was run down from the cold and a little lonely with John being gone all the time.

⌁ *Anna looked rested and remarkably good. I thought maybe the worst was* over, that the other things were just her way of settling into this old house and paying homage to those who had come before us. It was such a relief . . . But then, I guess I would have believed anything at that point, just because I wanted so badly for the weirdness and the sickness to end. What a fool I was.

I asked Anna if she wanted to get up and go watch the sunset. I had already packed a picnic. She asked how much time she had to get ready. I told her about fifteen minutes, or we would miss the best colors. She wanted to wash her face and change her clothes since she had been sleeping in them all afternoon.

In about five minutes, I heard Anna running down the stairs and through the dining room.

"Race you to the car!" she called, rushing into the kitchen. She sounded great, and suddenly it seemed that the weekend might be salvaged after all, in spite of the rocky start at lunch.

The picnic basket was full of crackers and cheese and apple slices. There were two splits of champagne that Anna had picked up at the grocery and two slices of bread pudding with raisins from breakfast. Anna was a terrific cook, even if lately most of her creations were odd and straight out of the pages of the 1917 *Wife's Best Companion* cookbook we had picked up at an auction.

I turned, smiling, in the direction of her voice and stopped cold. Anna was wearing a long white skirt and a pleated blouse with a lace collar and sleeves that gathered just below the elbow. A white net of some sort held her long hair like a pouch and was tied tightly at the nape of her neck with a ribbon. She carried a shawl over her arm, ". . . in case it gets chilly." I looked into her eyes, and before I could take a breath, I knew. It wasn't Anna who looked back at me.

I don't remember the picnic or the sunset. Once, not long ago, when we talked about all the events that unfolded in our life, John asked me about that afternoon. I didn't believe it had even happened, until he showed me a photo of us that he took that day. He had braced the camera on the picnic table, focused it and set the shutter for a time release. You can see the pier in the background. I'm grinning happily. He was right. I wasn't there.

The gardens looked great that summer. On Saturday mornings, John liked to sit on the front step with a cup of coffee and watch me weed. Entertainment comes easy in our small town.

We had worked magic with those neglected beds, and there were flowers everywhere. Morning glories grew thickly up a wooden lattice arch we put over the walkway. Roses bloomed in pinks and reds, and a circle of cannas stood nearly five feet tall in the side yard. There were herb beds outside the kitchen door and a cottage garden with cleomes and foxglove and cosmos flanking the front entrance. New bridal wreath spirea bushes softened the corners of the porch. I had planted them right where the "Walking Tours of Carlston" brochure said they used to be. I knew they would eventually grow to six or seven feet and be covered with white blossoms in the spring, just as they probably were decades earlier, before they became old-fashioned and were pulled out to make way for stylish but boring, boxy evergreens.

John was amazed we had accomplished so much in less than a year. He asked one Saturday if I knew why no one had planted anything around the house in decades. I hadn't a clue.

It's true that the soil was sandy because we were so close to the lake, but I could compensate by heaping on lots of mulch and peat. The maples cast a lot of shade, but overcoming that just took a little re-sourcefulness and creativity to figure out what grew without a lot of sun. It wasn't so hard.

I look back now and wonder why I never questioned this apparent gardening talent of mine. Though I always said I had a "passion for gardening," until we moved into Maple Hill, the biggest patch of ground I'd worked was a window box. I cut a peach-colored rosebud and held it out to John, smiling. I was so happy there, kneeling in the soil, knees cushioned by a piece of foam rubber, a cultivator in one hand and a pruning shears in the other.

Dig deeper.

I looked at John to see if he had heard it too. He had turned back to the newspaper and seemed undisturbed. I let it pass. The cold had left my ears plugged and ringing, and sometimes the combination seemed to translate as words on the wind. I heard lots of things these days. Suggestions, usually. Most often when I was alone and tired, which was most of the time. It felt foolish, but sometimes I tried talking back. Once I thought I yelled too forcefully. I felt my breath knocked out of me, and I fell backward into the side of the couch as though I had been hit in the chest. I wasn't injured, just perplexed and exhausted, so I went upstairs and took a nap. I knew John worried about me, and I thought it best not to tell him about the incident. I know, now, we were both keeping things from each other.

~ *Anna was remarkably patient and thorough as she worked with the dirt,* adding fertilizer, manure, mulch, whatever each bed needed. Sometimes she moved plants three or four times before she was satisfied they were in the right place.

That peach-colored rose she cut for me was perfect, right down to the drop of dew still clinging to the outside petals. I got up and took the flower, brushing her forehead with my lips. Her skin felt cool. I was growing used to her unusual appearance. The skirts, mostly long or midcalf, had become sort of a daily uniform, alternated occasionally with baggy trousers. She wore her long hair braided down the center of her back or pulled into a bun, and sometimes gathered at her neck with a large bow. And in spite of the gardening gloves she wore, she was forever scrubbing at her fingernails with a brush to get the dirt out from under them.

I watched as she turned back to her weeding. The sun had tanned her face and lightened her hair. But there were dark circles under her eyes from sleepless nights, and her cheekbones were more pronounced. Dr. Lind had switched medications again, this time prescribing an aerosol inhaler that sent magic spasm-stopping medicine into Anna's lungs, but kept her awake at night. When she did sleep, she often woke me with frantic mutterings that seemed to creep out of vivid, senseless dreams—dark images she had no memory of in the morning.

When I went inside to get another cup of coffee, an odd sensation hit me again. I stopped in the living room to see if something was out of place. Anna's unpredictable behavior made me edgy these days, and I couldn't tell if I was simply spooked or if something was really wrong. I looked around and noticed nothing out of the ordinary. The furniture hadn't been moved since the weekend I came home to find it completely rearranged and Anna muttering that we needed heavier curtains. There was a lamp on in the corner by the piano, and a small vase of flowers on the round plant stand next to the rocker. The couch was still against the far wall. In the opposite corner stood the curved corner cabinet that had been in my family for years, and next to it hung the photos of the James family. I looked at them again, reluctantly. Anna and I had never discussed their presence after the first day I saw them there. Like the old-fashioned clothes and endless pots of soup, the bad dreams and obsession with those who had walked these floors before us, the photos had been moved in my mind to the column of things I could not bring myself to discuss with Anna. I did not ask her why she took down our photos in the first place, and had never asked when she might like to put ours back up. I walked a precarious edge, worried that she would not think it strange to have our walls covered with the photos of dead people we did not know. I was afraid that I was looking for trouble, being unreasonable, and falling out of touch with my wife. I wonder, sometimes, if I had been more capable of bringing up this crazy stuff—perhaps we could have avoided a lot of anguish. I simply did not know how to deal with it. And the few times I tried to talk to Anna about any of this, I was met with a blank stare. Anyway, nothing seemed newly amiss as I looked around the room, so I tried to shake off the creepiness and get on with the afternoon. The peaceful lull lasted less than twenty-four hours.

This town hates me!

"This town hates me!" Anna yelled as she stomped her way across the front yard early the next morning. She had left her gardening and walked to the store to pick up a paper.

"You?" I laughed. "Everybody in this town loves you. What are you talking about?"

"They hate me," she said again. She was steaming.

I asked what on earth had happened. She said she had been snubbed. I laughed again because I thought this was a big joke. Honestly, this is a person people wave to when they drive by. She smiles at everybody. She picks bouquets for the joggers who pass by the house and compliment her flowers. People like her.

She pounded past me up the front steps and ran into the house. And that's when I noticed she didn't have a paper.

I was puzzled and hoping—you can't believe how much I was hoping—this might just be her version of a setup for a funny surprise. I followed her inside and called her name. She was already in the kitchen making a cup of tea. Not coffee. Tea. When did that start, I wondered. And where was the paper?

"What's up?" I asked.

"They wouldn't sell me a paper."

"Why?"

"They wouldn't even open the door to me. They hate me." She was rocking slightly from side to side, and her face was flushed.

"Anna, stop a moment and look at me . . ." Oh, dear God, those eyes. She stopped dunking her tea bag and seemed disoriented. I tried again. "Anna, the store doesn't open until eight, does it?" It was just a few minutes after eight o'clock now. It would have taken her about ten minutes to walk back from the store. Her hands were shaking.

"Yes, that's right."

"The store wasn't open yet, honey. But it should be open now if you want to go back."

"No. I'm not going back. I want to dig up some sod around the side porch for a new flower bed."

She abruptly dismissed the event and moved onto something else. Did I try to get her to talk about her irrational response? Heck no. I just watched in silence as she drank her tea and headed back outside.

Later that afternoon, I walked out to see how Anna was doing. The gardens were blooming beautifully—roses, coreopsis and spring daisies had replaced the tulips and daffodils that had blossomed in April and May from the bulbs she planted just after Halloween. Anna had a gift. That was the one sure thing in my life at home these days. It all looked remarkably familiar and comfortable, I thought, as though we had lived in the house for many years and I had seen it all before. Then I remembered the eerie sensation I had felt the previous day, and suddenly I knew its source. I *had* seen these gardens before. I went back inside, to the living room, where the photos of Jeanette's gardens hung on the wall. By selectively enlarging or eliminating those abandoned garden plots that had dotted the yard when we moved in, Anna was practically duplicating Jeanette's gardens. Bush for bush. Flower for flower. Jeanette's were older, bigger and lush, but the likeness was striking. Clever girl. She never told me what she was planning. When I asked Anna about it later, she looked at me distractedly and said she didn't know what I was talking about. End of discussion.

June had been warm, and just a few days into July we already had received two inches of rain. The Fourth was dreary, but we both wanted to watch our first Carlston Independence Day parade, so we donned umbrellas and rain jackets and stood in the warm downpour. It was great fun. I livened up the morning by proffering a thermos full of

31

spiked lemonade that we passed back and forth, and I was lulled into believing, once again, that the weird things going on were simply my imagination. It even crossed my mind that this might be Anna's way of tiptoeing slowly into menopause. What did I know?

We never got to that joint doctor appointment. Being on the road five days a week left little time to schedule a visit. Then there was the holiday smack in the middle . . . at least those were my excuses. Several weeks after my initial phone call to Dr. Lind, Anna spiked a temperature of 105 degrees, and the doctor put her in the hospital. The nursing staff tracked me down in Albany—that much Anna had been able to tell them—and I flew home immediately.

I remember looking at Anna when I got to her room that evening. She was pale—grayish, actually, despite the heat of the fever, and seemed terribly confused about where she was and who she was. I sat on her bed and held her hands. She was trying to talk, but the words that came out made no sense. I had been avoiding her eyes for weeks, but now I screwed up my courage and stared. They weren't blue. They weren't the eyes I had looked into for years. They were deep brown with yellow edges, and they held my gaze for several seconds. I wanted desperately to believe that a high fever and lingering illness could change a person's eye color. I smiled at Anna, but there was no response. I felt like she was willing me to look at her. I couldn't look away. I couldn't even blink. Then those eyes opened wide, as though they had fixed on something vital. With enormous clarity, they stared straight back at me. Anna began to speak.

"Dig deeper," she said. That was all. The voice seemed to come out of her skin. Anna closed her eyes, and I jumped as the machines that monitored her heart and lungs suddenly began to howl.

"Oh, dear god, Anna, don't do this," was the first thing that came out of my mouth. As though she had a choice. "Don't leave me, Anna. Fight this thing, please. Fight it." I realized I was shaking Anna's shoulders.

Two nurses ran into the room and pushed me aside to get to her. They bent over her, checking electrical connections, tubes, IVs, printouts, pulse, blood pressure. They yelled her name and tapped her cheek gently. They yelled orders and numbers to the nurse and intern who came running in seconds later. I couldn't understand anything they were saying, and Anna's skin was turning blue. Another nurse came in pushing a cart full of equipment. Someone started chest compressions, and Anna's limp body seemed to bounce on the bed like the desperate flopping of sucker fish I had seen old men catch and toss on the pier to die. I couldn't get that image out of my head. My ears were roaring with all the noise of the commotion, and I was terrified. Anna was dying right before my eyes. The nurses continued to call out orders and move over Anna with practiced precision. A doctor ran in. I pressed back against the wall to get out of the way and heard myself scream Anna's name over and over, as though my calling might bring her back. And perhaps it did.

Abruptly, Anna's vitals began humming along smoothly again, as though nothing had happened. Her color began to return.

Except for the chest compressions, the nurses had barely touched her. They hadn't had time to give her an injection or to use the defibrillator. They were checking everything, calling out pulse and blood pressure numbers, calling her name to see if they could get a response. They checked connections again, following the tubes and lines from machine to skin to make sure everything was attached as it should be and groping for an explanation. The doctor ordered a couple of tests to see if they could determine what had caused her heart to stop. Their conversations blurred in my ears.

The nurses stayed for several minutes, checking everything for a third time. Then, I guess, they remembered I was in the room, too, still holding up the wall and dripping with sweat. They assured me Anna was OK and said I could go to her. I took her hand and held it for a moment. Then I leaned over her, slid my other hand under her head and pressed my cheek to hers. It was the best I could do to hold her, given that she was strung like a marionette with a tube in her arm, a monitor attached to her chest and oxygen streaming into her nose. I told her not to give up, that we'd get this thing licked. I had never lied to Anna before, but this was close. The truth is I didn't have any idea whether or not we'd get it licked. I didn't even know what "it" was. I only knew now that the invasion in our life, so insidious and controlling, was beyond Anna and me. At this point, I was pretty sure that I, alone, had seen all of what this monster had to offer. It wasn't a virus or unresponsive bacteria. It had a brain and a will. And it was consuming Anna.

But I knew only half of it. Anna was keeping secrets, too.

33

Two

$\sim$ *I thought John and I were close enough to be able to talk about anything,* but actually, we had never been tested. I didn't know how to tell him about the voices. I was constantly running through lists of what I thought they might actually be—low blood sugar, little seizures, Joan of Arc syndrome, a stroke, madness. I didn't even recognize them as voices at first. I thought, perhaps, they were my own conscience.

Dig deeper. Dig deeper. There it would be again. At first it was a quiet voice, gentle and easy. I even smiled a few times after I heard it. I was thinking maybe it was my guardian angel. But then it got louder and more persistent, and it went from that to angry. Several times I re-member turning around to see if anyone near me had heard it, too. But of course, I know now, it was reserved for me. So I dug and dug and dug until my fingers were raw, and I had no clue what I was digging for.

I have little memory of the weeks that led up to the fever. And no memory at all of being in the hospital. John says it's because I wasn't there.

Four days after being admitted, two days after the crisis, my fever broke, and I came home. That I do remember. John was on pins and needles. But I felt great—the best in a long time. The voices had stopped. And that my heart had stopped, too? Well, that remained a mystery. Tests showed nothing.

When we pulled in the driveway, I asked John if he would come sit on the front porch with me and have a glass of wine. I wanted to celebrate. I had grown so tired of being sick, and I just wanted things to get back to normal. I thought maybe a little wine in the middle of the afternoon would do us both some good. John said it sounded like a fine idea, but he started fidgeting with stuff in the kitchen as soon as we walked in—straightening things on the counter, emptying the dishwasher, scrubbing out the sink. I took a bottle of wine from the refrigerator and opened it, took out two glasses and poured them full. John had just had a good scare, and I figured he was probably worried sick.

I told him I was OK. Really. OK. Finally. He said that was good. And he kept on scrubbing.

"Come on out for some wine," I asked him again.

"I'll be there in a minute," he replied. And he kept on scrubbing.

So I waited. He was so preoccupied, he didn't even realize I was still standing there a minute later, until I said his name, and he jumped.

He whirled around and started firing questions at me, staring someplace beyond my shoulder.

"What did we do on our first date?" he demanded.

"We went to see the movie *A River Runs through It*. Why?"

"What was my dad's family business?"

"They were carpenters . . . he was the third generation, I think."

"What color are your eyes?"

"Blue, like yours, John. Have you forgotten? Come here and look."

He leveled his gaze finally and looked at me. I could see him exhale, as though he had been holding his breath for a very long time. Then he took the wine glasses from my hands, set them on the counter and wrapped his arms around me. He kissed my hair and my face, my eyes and my neck, my shoulders, and held me close.

"Welcome home, Anna," he whispered. He was shaking, and I could tell he was crying. "I missed you."

~ *I didn't know how long Anna would be with me this time, and we needed* answers—even if we didn't understand the questions, yet. I cancelled work for the next month.

Taking myself off the road for four weeks was no big deal. I rescheduled appointments and told everybody I was taking some time off to be with Anna while she recovered. I loved the flexibility that

35

working for myself offered. The most compelling reason for staying home, though, was that I couldn't bear the idea of going away and coming back to those eyes. I guess I thought if I stayed with Anna every minute of the day, I could scare away the intruder—or whatever the hell it was that passed through our house and into Anna and was, apparently, taking a break.

A few days after Anna came home, I decided it was time to start talking. I wondered how it could be that this bizarre thing had happened in our life, and yet we had never, ever spoken of it. For that matter, I wasn't sure Anna even understood that anything odd had been going on. Dr. Lind said her virus had gone haywire. That it had, perhaps, suddenly reacted to something in Anna and multiplied, totally out of control. Then, like a flaring brush fire, it simply burned itself out before it consumed her. Whatever. I knew there was more. What I didn't know was whether Anna knew that too.

I had a tough afternoon trying to figure out how to broach the subject. I had forgotten how close Anna and I were before she got sick, and how easy it had been to talk to her about anything, so I over-orchestrated everything and nearly blew it. Anna had been feeling so good since the fever broke, and she had no sense of urgency to drag up the whole incident again. I didn't want to scare her, but on the other hand, I thought we needed to find out what had happened to her, beyond the virus theory. And I was certain, dead certain, that this wasn't over yet.

&· *John had all the makings of a romantic dinner—wine, cheese, grilled* peppers, tomatoes and beans from the market, Sara Lee carrot cake. A feast. It was early August and sticky hot, so he set a table and chairs under the big walnut tree in the backyard. If there was any breeze at all, we'd catch it there.

Liam and Karen Carson, our neighbors, came home from work and stopped by the side porch door to see how I was doing. John pulled a bottle of champagne from the fridge and asked them to join us. Though our paths didn't cross much, we liked the Carsons a lot. They never once complained when I decided to till up most of the backyard and plant it in flowers. They never raised an eyebrow when the owners of a dairy farm drove their manure spreader down the back alley and deposited ten cubic yards of composted cow poop at the end of the driveway so we could spread it over the gardens. We were nuts about their four kids, whom we hired to help us rake leaves and shovel snow.

When they left, John started the grill and poured the wine. He was so quiet, I should have guessed that something was up. But, truthfully, this whole thing with my illness and the hospital scare ... well, things were a bit strained between us, so the silence from my normally chatty husband registered only as yet another way our marriage had been altered by the events of the past year. When the food was ready, we took it to the picnic table and toasted. John started dishing out his perfectly cooked vegetables.

You probably don't need this much detail, but it's the way I remember it, moment by moment, like it was happening in slow motion. I can see it all when I close my eyes. I can hear every sound. It's all there ... everything John said, the reddish pink of his cheeks from the heat, a neighbor's dog barking one street over, even the way the wind suddenly picked up as it often does along the lakeshore in the late afternoon. I thought things were finally turning around and that the whole incident was behind us. It seemed like I had been gone a long time—much longer than a few days—and I wanted to remember every second, unfettered by the unidentified, nagging voice I was trying very hard to forget. I finally felt like I wasn't losing my mind.

John was dear but stiff. We chatted small talk for several minutes. It was awkward but OK. I expected it and figured it would take us a while to get back in sync. I knew that couples who go through something traumatic like a serious accident or a brush with death often have difficulty relating to each other in the months that follow. John told me I looked great and asked, for the one hundredth time, how I felt, and that was when I began to come unglued. Since I'd come home from the hospital, John had this habit of looking at me sort of sideways, like I wasn't supposed to notice that he was watching. It made me feel like he didn't trust what I said—like he was waiting for me to fall over in a dead faint or break out into a sweat. It really bugged me. I just wanted everything normal again. I had a short fuse, I guess, and it didn't take much to put me over the edge.

"John, for crying out loud, will you stop looking at me like I'm about to burst into flames!" I yelled at him. I knew I was in serious danger of ruining the dinner he so carefully put together, so I slowed down and reached across the table for his hand.

"I'm fine, honey. It's all behind us. The virus is gone."

I wish I could paint for you a picture of John's face at that very moment. It was so clear that he was devastated by something, and for the life of me, I couldn't figure out what it was. He was shaking his head slowly and staring at me, like he was trying to see inside me. And now I know, he was.

Finally, he spoke.

"Anna, what do you remember about the weeks leading up to the day you were taken to the hospital?"

I thought his timing was lousy. This was supposed to be a celebration of my health, not a rehashing of my illness. He was wearing me down. I wanted so much to tell John how frightened I had been, the compulsions I couldn't explain, and the days I had no memory of. But the fear, which I now know we both felt, had become a wall between us, and we had forgotten how to talk to each other. Right now, I just wanted to have a glass of wine, maybe three, and revel in feeling good.

∽ *How do you begin to tell someone that they had disappeared for periods of* time over the past year? How do you tell the woman you love so deeply that you think she is possessed and that something inside her is trying to take her? I thought back to the day I tried to talk to Dr. Lind about Anna's weird behavior. The list of strange occurrences had gotten longer, but I was no better equipped to talk about them now than I was then. I had been raised by a father who took great pride in his pragmatism, his firmly grounded sense of reality. We were not permitted to believe in ghosts. He did not even consider them an acceptable subject for scary entertainment. We did not trick-or-treat. We did not sit around the fireplace at night and tell ghost stories. And I was chastised for the mere mention of the possibility of aliens in my closet or monsters under my bed. That didn't mean I was never afraid. I just wasn't allowed to talk about it.

"Anna, I want to talk about some things that happened recently. While you were sick. Actually, I want to talk about you, sweetheart. You nearly died, you know, and I don't want it to happen again." Boy, did that sound stupid. I was groping. She dismissed it. In fact, she got up from the table and pretended to go inspect one of the new rhododendrons she had planted over Memorial Day weekend. She had her back to me, then suddenly turned. It was clear she was angry.

"Dr. Lind says the virus is gone, John, and I feel great. Look at me. Do I look so bad? What do you want? What the hell will it take to convince you that I'm OK?"

"There's more, Anna. That's why I want to know what you remember. Talk to me, please. . . . I want to know what was going on inside you, because you changed . . . I want to tell you what I saw. And what I heard. Anna, you don't know what it was like to watch you change, and to come home every week and be afraid of what I'd find. I couldn't tell anymore which one of us was going crazy. And in the hospital, Anna, it just wasn't you there, I could tell. I know you. And that wasn't you. We have to talk about this, honey. Please."

I was really stumbling. I tried to be gentle, but I felt like I wasn't getting through. She could be so hopelessly stubborn. There was a terrible silence between us. It was so hot, I could feel the sweat dripping down my chest inside my shirt. Dinner was mostly eaten, but the cake sat untouched. A fruit fly landed on the rim of my wine glass.

"Damn it, John, can't you leave this alone? It was nothing. . . ." She turned away again.

"It was nothing," she said, louder, to the trees. "NOTHING!"

Her hands were balled into tight fists and shaking at her side. The veins stood out on her neck.

I told myself, don't argue. Be quiet. Let her keep talking.

I got up and walked to her, so afraid that she would bolt, leaving me with nothing but my questions. The tension made me feel sick to my stomach. I wondered if this was what people meant when they described the turning point in their marriage—the precise moment they could feel it collapse. I wanted to touch her, to hold her, to make the memories of the last year go away, but instead, I stood there with my hands at my sides, frightened and useless.

I felt a breeze. Anna turned. God, I wanted to avoid that face, but she stared straight at me. With blue eyes. Blue eyes wet with tears, and she looked so damn scared. It was the last thing I expected of her. Anger, yes. But not fear. I remember hearing a squirrel off to my left digging in the leaves in the woods. A red-headed woodpecker was drilling for bugs in the old telephone pole in the alley. I could see Anna's hands opening and closing now, as though they were the only parts of her body she could move, and I fought the urge to take them in mine and apologize for bringing up this whole mess. I stood still and told myself one last time, be quiet. Let her do this. It was just Anna and me again—two people who loved each other, trusted each other and didn't keep secrets.

She shrugged and forced a smile. "Someone's been talking to me."

☙ *Over the next two days, John and I got out most of what we had been* unable to talk about over the last many months. He learned about the voices that rolled around in my head daily—and we decided that it was the same voice he finally heard in the hospital just before I flat-lined. We made silly jokes about my odd behavior that he had nearly become resigned to. He showed me photos he had taken of me with my hair pulled back and stuck in some kind of snood—no makeup, a shawl around my shoulders. But he never got a close-up picture of my eyes— the yellow-brown beauties that were his first clear clue that something was dreadfully wrong.

I knew about my compulsive digging and planting, moving plants from one spot to another, spading up patch after patch of sod, and my absolute obsession with the history of the house and the people who lived there. But neither of us had a clue about how any of that had come about or why. John was convinced that something had invaded my body. That was a bit hard to take from my matter-of-fact husband who never gave any indication that he believed in anything other than the here and now.

Trying to determine the identity of an alien presence is not something either of us had any experience with. In fact, it was a leap for us to even say the word *ghost*. We felt so stupid. We talked for days about where to go, who we could confide in. We made more jokes to ease our fears. I asked John if he had made love to me when I had brown eyes and if it was fun sleeping with a new strange woman.

"No to both questions," was all I got. He didn't even crack a smile. Guess he didn't think the idea of it was as funny as I did.

"OK. Here's the truth, Anna. First, you didn't show any interest in lovemaking for the last few months, so the issue never came up. Second, when my imagination went over the edge, I worried that maybe whatever was overtaking you was out to get me, too, so I stayed away. Remember the nights when I told you I was afraid you weren't sleeping well because of my snoring, so I stayed in the guest room?"

I guess we'd both seen too many scary movies.

40

In the end, our complete lack of experience with anything related to the spirit world led us to the phone directory, of all places, and to a New Age shop in Grand Rapids that resembled the head shops we had frequented in high school. We had driven by it a couple times in years past, and since we didn't have any other idea of where we might go to find someone to help us with a ghost, we started there. We thought maybe we would find books or tapes or even a community bulletin board with business cards thumbtacked to it. Can't you see it? "Work Wanted—Authentic séances, tarot card readings, confidential investigation of spiritual possessings. No job too small. Call for free estimates."

~ Instead, we found a seventeen-year-old girl with pink and black hair and more pierced body parts than I could count in one self-conscious look. She was dressed head to toe in black, had a fabulous body and was swaying to the strains of a woozy CD. I wondered where her mother was. I don't know what we expected. We said we were just browsing. God, we must have looked so out of place in our khakis and polo shirts, but she left us alone to study the books and oils and charms and music. Finally, I told her we were interested in information about trying to identify spirits.

"Do you have any books or anything on the subject?" I asked, trying to sound casual.

"Like ghosts? Nope. Sorry. Nothing like that. We mostly have, like, crystals and stuff to make your life nicer. Self-help books. Aromatherapy candles. Peace jewelry. Cool music . . ."

I wanted out. Anna already had her hand on the doorknob. "Any place around here you recommend for lunch?" I asked. The girl pointed to a store across the street.

"Go see Roberta. She makes sandwiches and salads and energy drinks and stuff, and she has a lot of —you know—herbs and stuff. She's very spiritual."

"What does that mean?" I asked. Snarled, actually. I was a little more gruff than I intended to be. Anna heard my tone and picked up the conversation.

"Thanks very much," she called out to the clerk. "You've been very helpful."

"No problem." Right.

ॐ *We walked across the street holding hands. I knew this was not something* John was very comfortable with—me either, for that matter, but we had to start somewhere. And it felt good to be close to him again. We opened the door to the Blue Sky Café and Apothecary and headed for the lunch counter. Behind it stood a woman I guessed to be in her late sixties, with long, wavy salt-and-pepper hair, deep brown eyes and a smile that was as welcoming as open arms.

The menu was pretty simple. There were soups and several salads, some sandwiches, cookies and muffins. John ordered a salad. I stood there numbly, looking at the handwritten list of the choices du jour on the chalk board. Nothing registered. The head shop had been an unsettling place, and hope was giving way to fear. I was so distracted I apparently didn't hear John ask me what I wanted to eat.

A gentle voice from behind the counter brought me back.

"How about a salad for you, too, with sliced pears and blue cheese? And I have fresh pumpkin muffins."

I looked at her and smiled. I could feel myself nodding. I didn't even wonder how she knew. She smiled back, looking from me to John for a few moments. Then she said, simply, "I can help you." And somehow, we knew she wasn't talking about food.

Roberta was our phoenix. I never did find out how we *really* ended up in her shop—if she had summoned us in some way, if our karma was particularly good that month. I keep forgetting to ask if she knew. Anyway, the reasons why were the last thing on my mind at the time. I didn't care. I only knew that someone else on this earth was about to share in the story of our bizarre first year in Maple Hill, and it appeared she didn't really need much explanation.

It unfolded so easily. There were no other customers around—it was a little late in the afternoon for lunch—but even so, I realized after Roberta went to the kitchen to get our food that the "open" sign on the door had been turned around. Just like that, we walked in, ordered, and she closed the store. When she brought us lunch, she sat down at the table with a cup of hot, fragrant tea and looked at us with the most peculiar, peaceful face I ever remembered seeing.

"What have you figured out so far?" That was how she opened the conversation.

John answered.

"Not much. That's why we went to the store across the street. We thought maybe we would find some books or something that could help us. The girl sent us here." John was pretty lucid at that point. I was still smiling and speechless. For no good reason, my fear was suddenly ebbing. Roberta reached across the table and cradled my face in the palm of her hand like a loving aunt might do. Her skin smelled like violets.

"You have been through a lot. I can see it. You both have."

I thought I might cry from relief. The weight of what John and I knew was now shared by three instead of two.

"You don't need books," she continued. "You have me, now. I can see some of your story but not all of it, so let's talk a while and find out what we know. Then we can go to work on the parts we don't know." There was that gentle smile again.

Roberta talked almost in circles, in a very simple way, perhaps so she wouldn't frighten or confuse us. It worked. We were in a fog. We hadn't even looked at our food. Roberta apologized for not having introduced herself. She got up and sort of hugged our shoulders across the counter, then said she was going to get us both something strong to drink, and she headed into the kitchen.

 What she came back with and put in front of Anna and me was the color of root beer and tasted like black tea laced with very old bourbon. It was odd and ice cold and very good.

"Please eat first," she urged us. "I love cooking for people, and nothing is more satisfying than watching people eat what I cook! You eat. I'll talk."

So we ate while Roberta chatted. She talked about the shop, about the six kinds of greens she puts in her salads—all locally grown—and about a recent shipment of freeze-dried morel mushrooms that she was itching to make into crepes. She refilled our glasses, brought a plate of cookies to the table, then gathered up our dishes and took them to the kitchen. She was, actually, an excellent cook. I mean, it's hard to screw up salads, but they were really tasty, and Anna reported the pumpkin muffins to be ". . . sensational!" She had two.

I don't know when or how the conversation changed from food to spirits—as in ghosts, not liquor—but it did. I realized quite suddenly that Anna and I were spilling our guts to someone who had been a total stranger an hour earlier. It made me wonder what was in the tea.

43

There we were, chatting away like old friends, laughing over the details of Anna's bizarre behavior. It was a good place to start because the reality of it all was bleak and frightening.

"So you got to be an expert on soups, eh, Anna? I'd love some of your recipes. Soup is a big seller, here, but it's not my forte. John, with all that marvelous food that Anna's been cooking up, why is it that you don't weigh three hundred pounds?"

"Anna's always been a good cook, even before the soup and bread phase," I told her. "That's why I have to have a job that takes me away from home every week. I diet for the four days I'm on the road, then come home and Anna spoils me again . . . it's a tough life!" I was relaxed, and Anna was actually smiling.

And then Roberta moved in like a tiger.

"Anna, when did you realize that there was something odd about your behavior?" It was a delicate shift and Roberta's first step into the serious zone.

"Not long after we moved in, I got real nervous about something I felt in the house," Anna began. "I couldn't put my finger on it, and I thought I was being silly and that I was just scared like I'd always been when I was alone in a house. So I tried not to think about it." Anna might have stopped there, but Roberta was still and fixed her eyes on Anna with great interest. She obviously wanted more, so Anna obliged.

"One day, I realized I was making bread . . . again . . . and I wondered when it was that I had taken such a shine to baking. And I was obsessed with gardening. I was planting and moving things like a crazy woman . . . But I seemed to find a reason for all of it, and I just didn't think about it much. The only thing I couldn't explain was the voice. It freaked me out a little, especially when I realized that John didn't hear it. I actually began to think it was something kind of special—like maybe I'd been singled out because I had particular sensitivities or something. I just didn't see how different I'd become. And toward the end, I don't even have memories of a lot of the things I did, or that John and I did together. What I don't understand is why couldn't I see that I looked like some old widow? What was I doing in those long skirts and pulled-up hair? And why didn't I think it terribly odd to take down the photos of my own family and put up photos of the James family?" Anna had barely taken a breath, but now she stopped and held out her hands and shrugged. She had so many more questions than she had answers.

"The James family?" Roberta asked.

"They lived in the house until 1919," Anna replied. "I found photos of them at the museum, and I had them enlarged and hung them up in the house where our own family photos had been."

"Ah, this is a good beginning," Roberta mused. "Now tell me everything from there on."

Roberta asked us about the lives of the James family, since they were clearly linked with Anna's actions. So we recounted all we knew about Jeanette and Martin, from their romantic Canadian beginnings to Martin's untimely death. It was dark when we left the café. I think we both felt an enormous sense of relief, but there was also the unmistakable queasiness that one gets when faced with the enormity of the facts. Roberta said Anna had been possessed. That, actually, was my word. Roberta put it more carefully and gave the whole grim situation more dignity. She said the spirit of the house had come to reside in Anna. Doesn't that sound special.

The big question we shared was why.

❧ *Roberta came to see John and me at our house three times over the next two* and a half weeks. She spent three nights each visit, leaving her young staff to run the café. She always brought a basket of treats—things like pumpkin muffins and fresh mangos for me, grass-fed beef and aged cheeses for John. She introduced us to herb teas. We introduced her to Chateau Nevermore.

Roberta put together clues the way a chef assembles the ingredients for a banquet.

"Suspend judgment," she told us. "Try to remember everything out of the ordinary that happened in the last year. We'll put all that together with what we know about the house, and we'll have some answers."

She made it sound so easy.

She smiled a lot. She touched our arms when she talked, and she took copious notes. We were a congenial group and close as old army buddies. She was good medicine for us. She was also an accomplished gardener.

Once the voices stopped, my drive to plant and replant dwindled, along with any interest in weeding, pruning, staking, feeding, and all the other tasks that had consumed me over the past several months. The only part I was still smitten with was picking flowers for arrangements.

So, I lamented out loud, I was a sham. I did not have a green thumb, and I was very disappointed. In truth, it was memories of the insistent voices that kept me out of the gardens. I could not separate the two, and I couldn't convince myself that they wouldn't start again if I began digging around.

Roberta had studied horticulture at her mother's elbow and had been passed ancestral knowledge of herbal medicine from an old neighbor she had befriended. On her first morning at our house, after a two-bottle evening of storytelling, I found Roberta on her hands and knees pulling weeds from between the tomatoes. She had already dead-headed the geraniums on the porch, pinched the impatiens and watered the wilting flower baskets.

I started the day apologizing for the general state of messiness in the gardens and was immediately interrupted.

"Anna! Good morning," Roberta chirped, with a levity I hadn't heard around the house in months. "This feels so good. I hope you'll indulge me. The café leaves me little time to putter, and that is exactly what I woke up wanting to do this morning."

I mustered up a ". . . help yourself." But there was more on my mind. I was feeling sorry for myself that morning, and depressed by the neglected and dying flowers in our gardens.

"It wasn't me who made the flowers beautiful, was it?" I was whining. "I'm not a good gardener after all."

Roberta stood up and rested her hands on her hips.

"Gardening comes from the heart, Anna. It's not so much a skill as it is a passion. You put a lot of work into these beds. Something compelled you to create all this beauty."

"But I don't want anything to do with it now . . ."

"And you don't care to bake bread or make pots of soup all day long, either. Sounds like someone loaned you their passions for a while."

That was a tough thing to hear so early in the morning. I stared out at the yard, and my eyes filled up. Roberta came to me and held my face in her hands as she had done that afternoon when we first met. She looked into my eyes—not at them, as we usually do with others, but deeply into them. I thought perhaps she would be able to see all the way inside me and find little bags of compulsions floating around. And that in so doing, she might also find tiny tags attached to them, like the cloth loops my grandmother had sewn into the clothes I took to camp: "This belongs to . . ."

"We'll find out who it was, dear one. And we'll find out why. Meanwhile, on a more serious note, what on earth does that winery put in their wine? I had the most amazing dreams . . ."

~ *Roberta moved around our house with the ease of an old friend. We felt no* need to entertain her, nor she us, though we were pretty inseparable. We spent hot days together at the beach and returned sometimes in the evening to watch the sunset. We took in a few auctions and caught enough fish for two pots of chowder and one big fish fry when we introduced Roberta to Liam and Karen and a few other friends.

On her second visit, Roberta brought recipes for zucchini bread and muffins, zucchini soup, zucchini omelets and lasagna, zucchini strudel and something she called zucchini guacamole. It hadn't taken her long after she first arrived to discover a prodigious number of the foot-long green squashes stacked like cordwood in our refrigerator. Our plants produced scores of them, and after we sauteed it, fried it and ate it raw with blue cheese dressing, Anna and I had run out of ideas. Anna said too much zucchini made her teeth squeak. To Roberta, the cache was a vegetable jackpot. Zucchini manna.

With Roberta, we laughed a lot—a new sound in our house after so many months of fear and silence. We drank cold wine and ate marinated artichoke hearts and double-cream brie with abandon. Anna slept soundly and put on a little weight. It was bliss, I want you to know. We allowed ourselves to relax and forget.

Near the end of her third visit, as dinner was winding down on Sunday, Roberta reached for our hands and said softly, "It's time to talk."

🍃 *While John and I were blithely enjoying these days of R&R, Roberta had* been putting together a game plan. She never let on. In fact, having her around gave us a great sense of relief and celebration so we could take the deep breaths we needed before we could move on. But now we knew, on that dead-calm August evening, that the time to find answers had come.

"There is a woman who is asking for your help," Roberta began. "I have heard her. She weeps for her child . . . a baby. Rose."

The house was so quiet. A storm was moving in from across the lake. The windows were open, but the only breeze I could feel came from the ceiling fan in the library. I heard crickets off somewhere in the grass. And I swear the lights flickered.

"Do you know this woman?" Roberta asked.

"It sounds like Jeanette," I replied, looking at Anna for confirmation.

"Yes, Jeanette. Would you get me the picture of her."

John went to the wall of "borrowed relatives," as he called it, and took down the copy of the photo I had made of Martin and Jeanette and their two children. He handed it to Roberta, who stared at it for a full minute.

The sun was down, and the damp heat in the room turned into a chill that started at the base of my spine and worked its way up my back, settling across my shoulders like a cloud enveloping a mountain.

"How did Jeanette die?" Roberta asked.

"Homeless and brokenhearted," I said, wondering where that came from. Roberta had heard the story before—the abbreviated version that spilled out on the afternoon we first met. "After Jeanette's husband died of the Spanish influenza, baby Rose got sick and then was kidnapped," I began. "Or at least that was Jeanette's story. But the town didn't believe Jeanette. Behind her back, they accused her of not taking care of the baby, of relying on her Indian remedies instead of taking the baby to a proper doctor. They assumed the child died and that Jeanette had just buried her somewhere. That's why there was little effort made to find her. Even though the police couldn't prove the baby was dead, they weren't interested in going on a blind chase to solve a kidnapping they didn't think happened."

"And so?" Roberta prompted.

"As far as we can tell, Jeanette became even more ostracized. She must have suffered so much. When we read the stories in the paper, it was pretty obvious that people thought she was guilty of negligence, and whatever friends she had made abandoned her. So here was this young woman who found herself an outcast, grieving for both her husband and her baby daughter, all the while still trying to keep this house together and feed and care for her three-year-old son, with no job and no support."

48

Roberta asked about Martin's parents. She wanted to know what they were doing while this whole scene unfolded.

Since I first heard the story, I had wondered the same thing. I came to the conclusion that they were afraid. To support their daughter-in-law would have meant risking their own reputation. Jeanette's father-in-law was an elder in the church. So they made a very uncharitable choice. They turned their backs on Jeanette, too.

"And then they took her son," added John. "They called the authorities and suggested that she was not capable of caring for him, and they offered to keep him. That was all the police needed. They came to her house one evening and handed her a court document ordering her to turn over Andre. I think she was probably too weak to protest."

"And maybe she knew what was to come," I added

"What do you mean?" asked Roberta.

I explained that Jeanette had become ill. We couldn't tell if she had the flu too, or if she was just giving up.

John suddenly got up from his chair. He had heard this part before, and he didn't have the stomach to hear it again. With tears in his eyes, he excused himself and went to get more wine.

I turned back to Roberta. "Three days later, the police returned to Jeanette's house. Andre missed his mother terribly, as you can imagine. The paper described him as inconsolable. He wouldn't eat, and he cried for hours. Jeanette's in-laws were having second thoughts and wanted to return him. I guess they bit off more than they had planned for.

"Jeanette didn't answer the door, but it was unlocked, so the police went in. They found her on the floor. She had on her coat and was close to death. They called for a doctor, but she passed before he got there."

"And Andre?" Roberta's mouth twitched as though it hurt to ask the question.

"The paper said he was with the police when they found Jeanette. He ran to her, and she was able to put an arm around him. According to police, she told him she had been on her way out to get him and bring him home. They had a few minutes together, and she died like that, holding him. It was a dark day for Carlston.

"His grandparents were given permanent custody, and Andre eventually adjusted to his new life. He was a good kid. He graduated high school here in Carlston, held a few jobs, nothing with any future, and enlisted in the army. I guess he was thinking of making it his career. The photo we saw of him in his uniform—the one I made a copy of—said he was discharged after several years as a POW. One article in the paper indicated that he had been shot by friendly fire during practice maneuvers. He came back to Carlston to recuperate, then asked to be sent overseas. Except for the discharge date, we have no other information."

It got real quiet again. Roberta's eyes were closed. I knew her well enough by then to believe that she was putting pieces together. She was also hearing and feeling things that John and I were oblivious to. I looked up and saw John standing in the doorway.

"Jeanette wants her name cleared." Roberta's eyes opened slowly, and she smiled at us. "She has been trying for decades to get someone to prove her story, but nobody listened. I don't think she meant to hurt you, Anna, but it's clear that she took possession of you and got your attention in ways she wasn't able to with earlier residents. Jeanette wanted so much to make you understand, and you were a receptive host. But I don't believe she wanted to hurt you."

Except for the fact that Anna and I trusted Roberta and had become very fond of her, this sounded like a lot of bullshit. Remember, she was trying to convince a guy who wasn't allowed as a child to believe in ghosts. Punishment for getting caught telling a "ghost" story was a good stinging rap across the behind from my father, who, by the way, debunked the whole Santa thing for me by the time I was two.

"Are you telling me Jeanette is a ghost and she's been walking around this house since 1919?" I was a bit agitated.

"Ghost is your word, John. You might consider her an unrested spirit. I think she is trying to get someone to prove her story and resolve the issue once and for all. What Jeanette doesn't seem to realize is that nobody in this town particularly cares anymore."

"And was Jeanette responsible for Anna's sickness?"

"Yes," said Roberta. "And again, I don't think she meant to hurt her, but Jeanette has carried her sickness with her. Anna, you just assimilated that part of her, too. The problem is that as long as she clings to this need to prove her story, she can't move on. And her present ethereal state likely limits her movement to this property—except when she became part of Anna. So she can't find out for herself what hap-

50

pened to her daughter. She probably didn't even know her son had been captured or shot until she heard you two talking about it. I'm sure she didn't know what became of him."

"And the weird clothes?" Anna asked.

"The kinds of things Jeanette was wearing in 1919. She did the best with what you had in your closet . . . 'the best' meaning that she was trying to find things to wear that were similar to what she would have been comfortable in ninety years ago. And she probably exerted some influence when you went shopping, which is why you came home with long skirts and blouses in the style of the early twentieth century."

"And my hair? My cooking?" Anna continued. "Oh, John . . . the voices. They were real. I wasn't crazy."

I took hold of Anna's hand and could feel her start to shake. She popped the question that had been sitting on my tongue, too.

"Is Jeanette still here, Roberta? Is she here right now?"

"Oh, yes." Roberta was certain.

"Then, why am I all right again? Why don't I hear her anymore?"

Roberta breathed deeply and folded her hands in front of her. "I believe it's because she realized she was hurting you, and because she finally got our attention."

John let go of my hand and reached behind him to the buffet. He grabbed four cordial glasses and a bottle of brandy and began pouring. When he had filled all four glasses, he lifted one and proposed a toast.

"To our guest, Jeanette. Welcome. Our home is your home," he grinned. I rolled my eyes. "If there's anything we can do to make your visit more pleasurable, please don't hesitate to ask . . . Really . . . just ask!"

That was exactly the levity we needed. Laughing now, Roberta and I each reached for a glass, clinked with John and drank down. John looked puzzled at the fourth glass that remained full and untouched.

"I guess Jeanette is a teetotaler," he began. "Well, I'll just drink this for her, then." And picking up the glass, he toasted into the air and finished the cordial in one happy gulp.

Three

🍂 *How does one go about trying to track down a kidnapped baby, especially* with a stone-cold trail that is decades old?

On Monday morning, John and I headed out in separate directions. I called the History Department at the college and made an appointment to talk to Doug Beecher, who taught Michigan history. I asked about the frequency of kidnappings in that part of the century, and I learned, of course, that they were rare. Occasionally someone wealthy was preyed on, when a kidnapper believed a tidy, untraceable ransom could be extracted. It didn't happen in Carlston.

We couldn't come up with a plausible reason as to why someone would kidnap Jeanette's baby—her sick baby—unless it was a child killer, and there weren't very many of them around, either.

Adoption wasn't very popular, except during the flu years, when families took in the children of dead family and friends. We knew that children were an asset to farm families. They could work long days and earn more than the cost and effort it took to raise them. On a farm, an extra child meant more hands to milk and weed and pluck. But babies—sick babies—were of no benefit at all. And the kidnapping of a sick child from a poor widow made no sense.

"Is it possible that Martin's parents arranged that, too?" Doug asked.

I thought about that. They didn't approve of Jeanette, but I couldn't imagine them to be so wicked that they would orchestrate the disappearance of their own grandchild.

"Well, here's a long shot," Doug began again. "Maybe they didn't take her, but somebody else did. What might you do if you thought your neighbor couldn't take care of her kids? Let's say you knew someone willing to adopt a baby. And let's say you didn't have much respect for a half-Indian woman whose husband wasn't around to protect her anymore. It might have been easy, almost noble, to spirit away the baby to a new home."

I could only stare at Doug when he suggested this. The thought was so foreign to me. It was crazy, but I tucked it away for further consideration.

John and I had spent the day trying to find some clues to what had become *our* mystery. We got home about fifteen minutes apart, ordered a pizza and spread out on the dining room table all the information we had gathered. There were photocopied articles, pages of handwritten notes and not much more, but by the time our large double-cheese extra-sauce, mushroom-and-pineapple special arrived (things really were getting back to normal), we had come up with several possibilities as to why Rose disappeared. John started.

"OK, suppose it was the worst. A pedophile. A sicko. He might have been a local guy who knew Jeanette was alone. He could have watched the house and taken Rose from the front porch when Jeanette went inside for two minutes to check on dinner. That's how long Jeanette told the police that Rose was out of her sight."

That was awful—the worst thing I could think of. Rose would probably have been dead within a day or two, and there would be no trail that we could follow. The guy would have dumped her somewhere or buried her. If she hadn't turned up ninety years ago, she wouldn't turn up now.

"I know this is hard stuff for you to hear, Anna, but I think we need to come up with every conceivable option before we automatically rule things out."

He had a point, of course, and I got a sudden brainstorm. "Maybe the police got him on something else later on, and he confessed to this, too."

John said he thought of that too. He had only begun to scratch the surface by looking through old newspapers, but the brief scanning he'd done revealed nothing.

"You know," he continued, "I don't think that's what happened. This town was as quiet and safe then as it is now—maybe even safer. And I think it's a slim chance that a baby killer was running around with no one knowing it." He asked what I had come up with.

I ruled out any involvement by Martin's parents. Even though they had Andre removed after Rose disappeared, kidnapping Rose would have been too risky and too mean, even for them. We knew that a lot of people in town felt that the kids weren't being cared for properly—the tone of the newspapers confirmed that. So I explained Doug's suggestion that someone—or some folks—with high and mighty intentions could have snatched Rose and sent her on to another family.

John didn't buy the theory. "How would another family explain the sudden arrival of an infant? What about legal papers?"

"Well, according to the histories," I told him, "the Spanish influenza left uncounted numbers of orphans in its wake. *Uncounted* is the key word here. Government services were overloaded trying to find homes for all the little ones, and orphanages were bursting at the seams. Foster families were notorious for turning their charges into underfed, overworked farmhands, but they didn't need or want babies. Offers to adopt the children of deceased parents were processed swiftly and without much ceremony. In fact, a lot of kids didn't even get adopted. They were just sort of assimilated into other families."

We sat staring at our papers, as though if we stared long enough, the answer would come to us.

"John, do you know Jeanette's worst sin?"

John looked puzzled.

"She didn't send the kids to Sunday school."

"So you think some well-meaning person . . ."

"Ladies from the church."

"OK . . . let's put it on the list, but I have a hard time believing somebody would have the nerve."

With that possibility on hold, we continued shuffling through copies of old newspapers and city documents and various other unhelpful transcripts searching for clues. Back and forth we went for a couple hours, coming up with scenarios of what might have happened on Jeanette's front porch on August 17, 1919. I had one last bizarre thought.

"Maybe Jeanette arranged it."

"Why would she have done that?"

"Well, she had to have realized that life would be hard for her kids in Carlston, and that unless her circumstances changed dramatically, they were going to have to move to someplace cheaper and smaller. Much smaller. Probably to a boardinghouse. And she would have to go to work. It's likely that the kids would have grown up to be shunned by their peers just as she was. I think she loved the children a lot. They were, after all, her only tangible connection to Martin, and I think she was a good mother. There's no real evidence to indicate she wasn't. She just had ways that were different from most other families in Carlston. So maybe she gave Rose away. Maybe she arranged the adoption with someone out of town, because she knew Rose would have a better chance someplace else. Think of it . . . that would really have been the ultimate sacrifice for a loving mother."

"But why the kidnapping story then?" John asked.

"Well, she had Andre's future to think of. A mother who gives away one of her children is going to be looked at with disdain by the community. But a mother whose baby is kidnapped may suddenly get people's sympathy. Maybe she was hoping for some support from the town . . . hoping they would rally to help her and take pity on her."

"If your theory is true, it backfired terribly. What a mess. But I don't think Jeanette would have been looking for vindication all these years if she planned the scheme herself."

John was right. The only thing we would prove if that was the case was that Jeanette was as manipulative as people thought. Just in a different way.

". . . and anyway, Jeanette would probably have a pretty good idea of where Rose had been living all these years. She might not have felt the need to stay behind here."

John's last thought sent a chill through me.

"John, do you realize what you just said? Rose was born in 1919. She could still be alive. Maybe Jeanette is hoping we'll find her and bring her back here." That was clearly a possibility we hadn't figured on.

John smiled. "Where do we go from here?"

"We do have to do this, don't we?" I was suddenly as tired as I could ever remember being. I didn't care about the history of the house or the reason Jeanette had stuck around. I just wanted to go to bed. It was after midnight, and we had been scrutinizing our meager pieces of information for more than six hours. We had come up with a long list of possible scenarios that characterized Jeanette as everything from saint to sinner, as they say. I couldn't even remember anymore what were facts and what we had conjured up to fill in the gaps.

"Yes, but not tonight. How about a glass of wine?" John asked.

"That's what's been missing from this evening! Please, will you bring it to me upstairs? I've got to get to bed. I'm beat."

"Absolutely," he said, leaning over to kiss my face. I knew this was hard on him, too. "You head on up. I'll get the lights down here and be up with two glasses of Chateau Mellow in a couple minutes."

When John put the wineglass on my nightstand, I realized I had fallen asleep. In fact, nearly a half hour had passed since I had crawled into bed. John stroked my face and smiled at me. He had a bandage on his hand.

"What happened?"

"Sorry I woke you. It took me a while because a bottle of wine slipped out of one of the cases, and there was glass and wine all over the floor."

"One of your cases in the basement?"

"Yes. I wonder if the change in seasons makes the earth shift a bit under this house. I thought after one hundred years it was done settling. I'll check the rest of the boxes in the morning. Anyway, I didn't want to leave the mess there. Most of the wine got soaked up by the sand and dirt on the floor, but I started picking up the broken glass, and a piece slipped and cut me. No big deal. Still want your wine?"

"Of course, especially now that you shed blood to get it for me."

"You're such a romantic!"

I sat up and propped some pillows behind me. I asked John if it unnerved him a little to know that Jeanette was there with us.

"I try not to think about it. Except, you know, having two beautiful women in my bedroom at the same time has always been a fantasy of mine . . ." He screwed up his face into a sort of dirty-old-man leer that made me laugh. No matter how hard he tries, John cannot pull off being a jerk.

"Jeez, John. That first night we spent in the house when we made love on the parlor floor. . . . do you suppose she was watching?"

He laughed. "I don't know. And what about all of our wonderful

56

nights since then?" He headed to the bathroom, and I heard him toss his clothes into the hamper and brush his teeth.

"That gives me the creeps," I remember whispering to no one in particular.

John slid into the bed beside me and put his arm around me, pulling me closer. I loved having him at home. We sipped our wine in silence. He was right about the seasons changing already. It was a cool night and windy. In less than a month, we'd probably have our first snow. I wondered if Jeanette ever got cold. I wondered if she minded that I had taken down the photos of her family and put ours back up. Except for baby Rose. Darling little baby Rose, lying there in her handmade sweater with tiny pearl buttons and no idea of what was about to happen to her. Sweet Rose.

Four

&. *John didn't actually stop working altogether. He had been at the business of* wine long enough that he'd seen and solved a barn's worth of crop problems and could often help the winemakers with a conference call or two. But we did hire a young man, Peter, to handle orders for supplies. That was one area that John just didn't want to let up on, as he'd made a reputation for being able to provide unusual and ancient parts for wine-making equipment that vintners often couldn't find anyplace else. John was big on service, and his prices were fair, so his customers seldom found the need to look elsewhere. Nevertheless, John didn't want to give them a reason to start.

Peter is a prize. He is the son and heir apparent of a winemaker in northern Michigan, so he's grown up in the business. Peter was a student at Columbia University until he broke his leg in a nasty fall while rock climbing during a vacation in Colorado, and his doctor recommended that he skip fall term classes. While he was casting about for some kind of work that would keep him off the leg but not bore him to distraction, he called John looking for suggestions, not knowing that we needed help. His timing was perfect, and his learning curve was blissfully short. It was a simple matter of routing John's calls and faxes to Peter's home in Jordan Lake. Besides knowing just about everything there is to know about wine making, Peter has a great sense of humor, and he's as likeable as a puppy. The four-pound cast on his leg and the prospect of getting several months behind in his studies didn't even make him grumpy. Sales actually went up that first month that Peter was in our employ. It probably didn't hurt that he was majoring in business. He's one smart kid.

I headed back again and again to the library and the maritime museum to see what I could dig up. Now that we knew that the unresolved kidnapping was the root of our problem, I wanted to see if I had overlooked some small detail that might lead us to baby Rose. John had suggested that we put an ad in Carlston's weekly paper to see if anyone was still around who remembered the story firsthand. But after ninety years, we would be dealing with the memories of people who were just children themselves when it happened. I half considered seeing if I could go through old church records—perhaps minutes of the elders or ladies' prayer groups to see if they had been so bold as to record such a heinous deed for posterity. After several minutes of wondering how people could be so self-righteous, I reminded myself that we had no proof that the church had any involvement . . . and that I better redirect my thoughts to something less prejudicial or I might miss important evidence to the contrary. But you can see that I had quickly become judge and jury.

After John and I realized that Rose might be still alive, I felt an urgency to find her that kept me going seventeen hours a day. The wild dreams that I'd had earlier stopped, but they were replaced with endless hours lying awake thinking and thinking and thinking . . . trying to figure out what stone we could turn over to find the answer as to what really happened on our front porch in 1919.

The idea that Rose might be alive made me think, of course, that Andre might be, too. They would both be in their nineties, not at all an unreasonable age to expect these days.

I went back and read all the newspaper editions for several months following Jeanette's death, hoping that out of embarrassment for their shamelessly inadequate investigation of Rose's disappearance, they would have reopened the case. I thought Jeanette's death might muster some public outcry, some sense of . . . Lord . . . I don't know . . . some sense of duty, I guess. I couldn't get that picture out of my head of Jeanette, dying on the floor, holding her son, so desperately sad. And little Andre crying his eyes out hour after hour at Martin's parents' house. It broke my heart. Surely, I thought, it might have moved the hearts of the men on Carlston's police force, too? Or maybe some detective who would have been called in on the case.

Well, apparently none of that happened. There were no more stories. There was no reopened investigation. The house remained untouched for a while, until it was determined that Andre was the sole heir. Then the house and land were put up for auction, contents and all. And let me tell you, there wasn't much interest in this place—the house that had belonged to a dead heathen half-Indian woman—the place, in fact, where she died. There were dozens of curious onlookers but few bidders. It was a grim day. The newspaper said there were several pieces of furniture, dishes and personal items that no one would even bid on. The auctioneers kept grouping things together—a nice lamp with two armchairs, the wool rug with the kitchen table—hoping they could generate interest and get rid of everything. The owners of the boardinghouse bought several things, including Jeanette's bedroom set, but lesser items and all of the clothes were either given to what was then called the "poorhouse" or carried off to the dump at the end of the day. The house went cheap. When it was over, funeral bills, taxes and the mortgage were paid. What little remained went to Martin's parents as custodians of Andre. Jeanette's wedding ring had been removed and given to them, presumably so Andre could have it when he grew older. We wondered what became of it.

And that was that.

Well, at least until we moved in.

I take that back. Without giving all the details of our own experience, we talked with other neighbors in the weeks that followed, to see if they had ever heard about weird happenings in the house from previous owners. Nobody used the word "haunted," but they did say there was talk of odd things that happened occasionally in the house. And there were all those dug-up weedy beds that dotted the yard when we moved in. Did Jeanette talk to other owners ? Who knows?

∼ *In the midst of our search for Rose, Anna and I discovered the probable* reason why there were no gardens around the house. It seems that for years, the townspeople whispered the rumor that Rose was buried somewhere on the property. We guessed that local residents kindly passed on the story to every new owner, who then perpetuated the fraternity of reluctant gardeners. I guess nobody wanted to dig flower beds for fear of running into the remains of the tiny body. No sense of adventure. In a weak moment, I remembered the bones I had dug up in the backyard earlier, when I was turning the dirt for another patch of perennials. We had decided they were the leg bones of pigs—thick and short. Karen told us that old records indicated our yard had been a dumping area before any of the houses in the neighborhood were built, close to 140 years earlier, so we assumed that someone had simply dumped the remains of their slaughtered hogs there. It was, as I said, in a weak moment that I recalled the bag of old white, brittle bones that I had stashed in the garage for no particular reason, and I went to look at them again. They were huge—much too big for a six-month-old child. When I told Anna that night what I had done, she laughed and told me she had looked at the bones again, too. It was a good confession for both of us. We poured some wine, and toasted, once again, to Jeanette, and to our dear friend Roberta, who we believed was bringing us out of the dark.

One night after dinner, I was sitting on the couch reading our weekly newspaper and thinking how much we had let the house go in the last month. Nothing had been dusted or vacuumed, and we had stopped folding our clean laundry. It went as a jumble directly from dryer to drawers. I started to chuckle a little. Neither of us was particularly fastidious about that sort of thing, but still, I was surprised at the mess of unfinished projects and undone housework that surrounded me. Our focus on finding Rose had usurped our interest in nearly everything else. I couldn't remember the last time we'd invited Liam and Karen for dinner, and there was a stack of overdue movies rented from the library that we'd never even watched.

My eye was drawn to the photo of Jeanette that was still sitting on the floor, leaning against the wall. It was a perfect example—we had never rehung it after taking it down for Roberta to get a closer look, and didn't put it away after we took down the other James family photos. I bet we had walked past it two hundred times since that evening. From that distance of about eight feet, the woman's face that looked back at me suddenly seemed familiar, and I realized why. Anna was reading in the library, so I picked up the photo and carried it in to show her.

"Aside from our friend Jeanette, does this look like anyone you know?" I asked, pointing.

Anna was quiet for a moment, and when I started to give her a hint, she interrupted with a sudden "WOW."

"John, it looks like a young Roberta. Why didn't we see this before?"

That was what I noticed, too: the large dark eyes, high forehead and cheekbones, full lips. Jeanette had Roberta's features, or the other way around. If Jeanette had lived to be seventy, she could have passed for Roberta's sister. As it was, Jeanette, who was barely in her twenties when the photo was taken, looked like Roberta's daughter. We decided to ask Roberta if she'd seen the resemblance, and if her ancestors included any French Canadians. Nice idea, but it was one more of those things that got put on the back burner and finally dropped from the to-do list altogether.

I'd like to tell you that I felt great, and that all the weirdness we experienced throughout that first year had disappeared, that John and I were living examples of marital bliss again, blah blah blah. Though you might want to believe that as much as I did, it was not, of course, true. It is true that I did not hear voices anymore. I stopped wearing long skirts to the grocery store and—sorry, John—I left bread baking to the bakery. My eyes were blue.

But knowing that Jeanette was there in the house with us profoundly affected our life from day to day. I felt, sometimes, like I was living in a church or maybe catacombs. You know that feeling you get when you walk into an old cemetery, and there is a sort of stillness that has settled in that just shouldn't be violated? That's how I felt. Jeanette was everywhere, and not because she wanted to be, but because she couldn't leave until the whole mess was resolved for her. She was in her own personal limbo.

I wanted to talk to her. I wanted it so much that I spent hours camped on the couch trying to make a connection with this woman who was all around me, yet nowhere. I wanted to touch her face, to hold her hands, to comfort her and reach out to her in the way that the people of Carlston should have in 1919—to make up for their stupidity and ugliness. I wanted her to know that if I could have been there, I would have defied the townspeople and hollered until a proper investigation of Rose's abduction was carried out. I would have offered to give Andre a loving home.

62

In truth, it is only in the last few years that my friend Amanda has taught me to take the local government to task—as she would say, to "hold their feet to the fire" on important issues. In truth, and I hate to say this, I might have ignored Jeanette's plight just as the rest of the town did. In all my checking of newspaper articles, letters, any documentation of the events, I never learned of anyone who came forward on Jeanette's behalf. Not a single person. I cannot imagine how dark the world looked to her. In fact, I can barely talk about it even now without getting overwhelmed by a deep sense of anguish. I feel ashamed for this town. Yet, sometimes I understand their response so well that I am ashamed of myself. Fear can be overwhelming. And while there was so much we did not know about Jeanette's situation, what we did know was that the town was afraid of her differences, afraid of her influence, afraid for her children. We are not usually at our best when we operate from fear.

It was time to bring someone else into our private circle. Grace Booth had helped me find a lot of background on the James family when I was first searching out the history of the house. She had become a good friend—in fact, it was she who gave the thumbs-up to our checking out the New Age bookstore in Grand Rapids when we asked her about it, though she had no idea of the real impetus behind our going there. ("Any good, funky bookstores in Grand Rapids that you recommend we visit if we make a trip over there . . . ?") Grace's experience working at the library made her a tremendous resource, but she was also one very nice person, and someone I could trust with our story.

It was Grace who suggested a step in the search that was so simple, I was amazed we had overlooked it.

"You could put out a press release," she threw out casually.

It was cold that morning. We were sitting at the kitchen table looking through the piles of stuff we had gathered and wondering how to fit them together. Every time we did this, I was reminded of one of those jigsaw puzzles that is all one color, no picture, no logical place to start. I had my hands wrapped around my coffee cup for warmth and was a million miles away.

"Anna?"

I looked up and realized Grace was talking to me.

"A press release," she repeated. "We could send a press release statewide and see if we get any response."

She got my curiosity up. "What would it say?"

"Well, let's see." Grace reached over for a thick tablet of paper and began reading as she wrote. "Dateline: Carlston, Michigan. A young woman in this remote lakeside town claims to be possessed by a spirit seeking information about her daughter who she believes was abducted from her front porch in 1919 . . ."

"Oh, that's a great start," I said, trying to figure out if Grace was serious or pulling my leg. "First off, nobody is going to print that, and if they do, I'll have every phony psychic and Ouija board player in the state knocking on my door. Any other brilliant ideas?"

"Ouija board. . . . wow, Anna, I haven't thought of that since I was about twelve and got scared out of my wits at Betsy VanderHyde's slumber party," Grace laughed. "We spent the evening eating too much pizza and asking the Ouija board a ton of questions. By about one o'clock in the morning, I had a tummy ache from all the food, and I imagined ghosts hanging out in every nook and cranny in Betsy's house, so I called my parents and asked them to come get me."

"And did they?" I asked.

"Sure. I ran outside and met them in the driveway still wearing my flannel pajamas. And they let me sleep in their bed with them that night, which was the best slumber party of all. I wonder if Mrs. Vander-Hyde realized there was one less girl at breakfast the next morning. I never went near Betsy or a Ouija board again. But you know, Anna . . . I'd be willing to try it again if you think it might give us some answers."

During the first months that we lived in Carlston, when Grace had helped me find information about Maple Hill, I knew her only as someone very pleasant, helpful and efficient. She had been generous with her loaning of historic documents and seemed nearly as eager as I was to find out more about our house. She is devoted to the details of history. But when I invited her over and told her, in confidence, the whole story of our last year and Jeanette and all, well, a whole different Grace appeared before me. She was so funny when we were working together. I mean, she cracked these one-liners like they were written for her. When she wasn't being outright comical, she had a desert-dry sense of humor that I usually mistook for total cluelessness until I learned to read her better. Sometimes, Grace would look at me with a remarkably blank face as though I had said something she didn't understand, and when I started to explain, with simple words and inflection like I was talking to a child, she'd level her eyes at me and let fly with a zinger. She also has a wicked-good laugh, and during our search for Rose, she would often tell these wild stories about her childhood—like this slumber party stuff. I couldn't tell what was real and what was made up for my benefit, but I didn't really care. She kept me on track and filled our kitchen with laughter. She is a gem of a friend.

"Are you nuts?" It was all I could think of to say. I was picturing Grace and me huddled over a tattered old Ouija board, fingers lightly on that little hovercraft as it sailed across the board spelling out the names of the men we would love, the number of children we would have and the coordinates of Rose's burial site.

Grace's jaw dropped. She has learned to do that very well, too, and it's always a giveaway that what she says next will be silly.

"Me? You're accusing ME of being nuts? May I remind you, dear lady, that *you* are the one who talks with ghosts . . . I'll bet you still *have* a Ouija board."

"Oh, low blow," I said, feigning total hurt. "Even if it is true. And you just better be careful. Maybe I'll put a spell on you and turn you into a chipmunk."

"That's what witches do, Anna, not ghosts. And you are definitely not a witch. The most outrageous thing I think you're going to do to me is make me fat by forcing me to work long hours surrounded by plates of pumpkin bread and cashews, and following that with a veiled threat to order the all-you-can-eat fried perch for lunch at the Dunes."

Food. The Dunes! Grace had come up with another stellar idea. The pumpkin bread I'd put out for us that morning was long gone, and I realized I was famished. With her daughter in day care until late afternoon, Grace would be able to continue our work for several hours, so I agreed to take a break and go get lunch. I asked Grace to bring her pad of paper. The news release was really not a bad idea. In fact, I was beginning to think it was very good. By the time lunch was over, I was convinced that we'd have this whole story resolved in a matter of days. I guess that's the way I am. I can go from complete nonbeliever to missionary zealot in about twenty minutes, and then, look out. Once converted, I dog an idea like a hound on a fox trail. John, I think, already told you that.

A word about the Dunes. It sits on a small side street that runs down to the beach—an old two-story clapboard house with a wraparound porch, several fireplaces and pine-plank floors. If you're new to the area or feeling fancy, you go in the front door and get seated in the living room or dining room. They're both pretty, with their assortment of old tables and chairs, and buffets and hutches that hold napkins and silverware and extra coffee cups. Nothing matches, but it all works.

If you've been around at all, you know enough to go in the back door, which takes you right into the cavernous kitchen where there's almost always a few empty chairs at the big harvest table, or at the little café tables set up in the adjoining four-season porch added in the '80s. And if you know enough to go in the back door, then you also know to stop at the old Hoosier cabinet and pour yourself some tea or coffee or lemonade. If it's lunchtime, you can help yourself to a formidable hunk of cornbread from the glass-covered cake plates. Sometimes there are muffins left over from breakfast—they are big and perfectly undercooked—slightly gooey inside with a crusty outside top. I have awakened in the middle of the night with a craving for these oven masterpieces. In the evening, you're likely to find a big cutting board out on the harvest table with pieces of focaccia bread smeared with goat cheese, sliced tomatoes and basil or bruschetta with black olives and artichoke hearts. Owner Gina Tartelli makes the best food in the world and lots of it. She's about five feet eight inches and weighs in at 130 pounds (I asked), and every time I see her she's nibbling on something. Why she isn't round is beyond me.

Gina is actually the biggest reason to go in the back door. She's likely to be behind the stove, standing at the elbow of one of her cooks, and she's usually in the middle of everything, stirring a tricky sauce or flipping an omelet, or both. There's a good chance she'll come over to greet you, or at least yell hello, whether you're a longtime back-door friend or a new one. By the third or fourth visit, you'll find yourself on the receiving end of a big hug or a compliment or both.

"You're looking so pretty, Anna," she sometimes says. Or "Hey, girl, cool jeans! You get those around here?"

She also kisses all the babies and hands out lollipops to anybody who looks younger than eighteen. Why she's fifty-eight and has never married is anybody's guess. Did I mention she also has a pound of curly black hair and a face like a Madonna?

On this particular afternoon, we walked in the back door, poured ourselves coffee and walked to an empty table on the sunporch. I picked up a carrot muffin en route. The place was empty. It was mid-week and a little early for the lunch bunch, which was fine with us. Grace ordered the perch special, and I asked for the black bean salad, which Gina makes with grilled red peppers, lime juice and ginger. And her homemade mayonnaise. See what I mean? Good stuff. We also ordered Lillet—a lovely little French aperitif we were introduced to here, which I usually reserve for celebrating long weekends. Gina serves it ice cold with an orange slice at lunch.

The restaurant has been around for nearly one hundred years. Gina says that when she bought it ten years ago, the only thing she changed was the menu. And, actually, it's the ingredients that have changed more than the names of the dishes themselves. She still serves hot turkey and gravy sandwiches, only the turkey is raised locally and roasted in her ovens, the gravy is rich and lumpless, and the organic potatoes are mashed in their skins. Her meatloaf is made with venison and dried cherries. And Gina thinks canned vegetables are next of kin to poison.

It took the locals about two days to realize Gina was the best thing to hit Carlston in a long, long time. They even forgave her for making the entire restaurant "no smoking."

Just before we ordered, we called to see if John was home yet. He'd been out that morning taking care of some wine business. He answered the phone and said he was hungry and ready for a break, too. When we hung up, we put in our orders, which came to the table just as John pulled into the parking lot.

Gina came out to give John a hug, slid her slim arm around his shoulders and escorted him to the table.

"Two lovely ladies, just like you ordered, dear!" She kissed his forehead and giggled at her own joke as he sat down.

"Two lovely ladies *and* fresh perch? My, this *is* my lucky day!"

"Just be sure you put the tartar sauce on the fish, John, not on the ladies."

"Right. Thanks, Gina. And I see you've been getting them a little drunk?"

"Primed, dear, just primed." Gina and John are crazy about each other, but that's the kind of ribbing Gina gives all her favorite locals. I honestly think she could go back to serving instant mashed potatoes and canned green beans, and the restaurant would still be crowded every day.

"Hey, guys, what do you think of the new furniture?" Gina pointed to an old chalk-blue pie safe on the porch that held stacks of serving platters and coffee cups. It looked about a hundred years old and had the rounded edges you would expect of a well-used cupboard. Perfect for the Dunes.

"Nice, Gina. Where did it come from?" Grace asked.

"I got it at an estate sale last weekend," Gina said. "At White Gables—that big old cottage down the street from you guys," she said, looking at me. "The owners are selling, you know, and they had a ton of stuff that had been in the house forever. They called me and asked if I wanted a sneak preview. The Helmstaads built that place before the turn of the century. They just kept passing it from generation to generation. This is the first time it's ever been offered to the public. I don't know how they could do it . . . but the kids have moved away, and there's nobody to pass it on to. And, dear God, you should have seen the furnishings. Family heirlooms that nobody wanted. Karen Helmstaad said her grandmother bought the pie safe for next to nothing at an auction in 1919 . . . Anna?"

I had barely heard the last of what Gina said. A chill had started at the base of my spine as soon as I saw the piece, and without realizing it, I had risen from my chair and started across the room toward it. I remember sliding my hand across the top, which was rough and cool to the touch, and then I reached down to unlatch the right-hand door.

"Anna." I heard John say. It was not a question. It was a plea.

I turned the latch. The door opened. And there, inside on the wooden door, were the primitive, barely discernable scratchings of a precocious child who was learning to write the initials of his name: AJ. Andre James.

∼ When Anna reached down to touch the letters, Andre's name spilled out in a whisper. She turned to me with the most quizzical look on her face, as though she didn't quite comprehend what she was seeing. But, of course, she knew exactly what it was. Then she went pale, and I thought she was going to pass out. I had already left my chair and was walking toward her, so I picked up the pace a bit, reached out and wrapped my arm around her waist as she steadied herself.

"Hey there, baby. A little too much Lillet so early in the day?" I asked, trying to make light of what had just happened. Then I made some stupid comment about her tuna getting cold and steered her back to the table.

I'll never forget Anna's face at that moment. Forgive the sports metaphor, but I saw it once on a fullback after he intercepted a magnificent pass and ran the ball back sixty yards for a touchdown. He had scored brilliantly, but remembered a moment later that his team was still down by forty-six points with three seconds left in the fourth quarter. It was the agony and the ecstasy in reverse. Grace, who sized up the situation in seconds, didn't let on that anything odd had happened. When Anna got back to the table, Grace pulled out her chair and announced cheerfully, "Anna, how cool! You found a piece of Jeanette's furniture. What are the chances of that?" And then, "Sweetie, you are a cheap date! One drink and you get rubber knees!"

Gina, meanwhile, understanding none of this, looked moderately alarmed and hurried off to the bar after running a hand along Anna's forehead, checking to see if she was warm. She called over her shoulder that she was going to get some ginger ale.

"I'm OK," Anna responded, wrapping her arms around me for a brief moment. Our eyes met, and I smiled, and she smiled back, and I knew she was OK. She sat down, and that marvelous brain of hers kicked into gear.

"John, it's possible there are other pieces of furniture still in Carlston that came from that auction. And maybe the people who own them know something about Rose. Maybe their grandparents passed down the furniture and the story to go with it!"

The discovery of a piece of furniture that had belonged to Jeanette was exciting and spooky at the same time. As if the story of the auctioning of the Jameses' possessions following Jeanette's death wasn't real enough, we now had a pie safe in our midst that had survived that sad day, passing from the Jameses' home to the Helmstaads'. I think we realized right then that we would never see another antique in someone's house in Carlston without wondering if it had been Martin and Jeanette's. We also understood that Jeanette was apparently still close enough to Anna to be able to draw her to the cupboard and propel her to open it. At least we assumed that's what happened. I don't know. Maybe Anna just put two and two together really quickly and decided to open the door and see what was inside. But she thinks not. Anna doesn't remember getting up from the table or even opening the

69

door. She just remembers seeing the image of a child with a blunt nail in his hand and a smile on his little face, drawing a surprise for his mama.

❧ *I really was fine. Seeing the initials was a shock. Nothing more. Between* that and the midday drink, I got a little dizzy. I'm sure Gina thought I was pregnant. Lunch was good, and I *was* very hungry. Gina had other guests to fuss over, and the afternoon proceeded without further oddities. Over warm apple crisp, Grace and John and I agreed that going down the furniture-investigation path might yield some information, but, like trying to pick the memories of locals who were around in 1919, the facts would be old and could be altered by years of repeating, forgetting and filling in the blanks with borrowed details.

I brought up Grace's idea to send a news release, and John jumped on it immediately. We also voted three to nothing to table the Ouija board suggestion till later. Much later.

By the end of September, I was feeling my perennial nostalgia that always comes on with this last, brave, boisterous season. Autumn excites me, makes me feel like time is running out with so much to accomplish before the ground freezes. Before Halloween, I had canned fifteen quarts of tomatoes, picked bushels of herbs to dry, made hot pepper jelly until the tips of my fingers were raw from slicing jalapeños without gloves and made several bottles of raspberry cordial from a recipe I wrangled from a friend. It's pretty easy. Raspberries, vodka, sugar. Mix. Wait. Drink. Half the fun is testing each batch to see if you got the proportions correct. What could be simpler? And that fall, I was looking for simple.

Grace had the patience of a greyhound. She had laid low for days and didn't bug us about the release, even though we had agreed, back there at Gina's, that we would write one. Not should or could, but would. And soon. Grace was poised to run with it as soon as we gave the OK. And that, I guess, is where the fear began to creep in again. John voiced it first.

"What kind of nutty people are going to call us when they see this?" he asked, with his standard when-all-else-fails-consider-the-worst-case-scenario approach. I started rubbing my eyes, then my eyebrows and my temples. I slid my fingers up under my hair, let out an exasperated sigh and finally just dropped my head in my hands.

"Maniacs," I said, looking up. "Maniacs, John. Ax murderers. Perverts. Bored old ladies. Fortune seekers. Hollywood directors. Damn. How do we sort out the directors from the fortune seekers?"

"Wear your bathing suit," John said.

"What?"

"Wear your bathing suit," he repeated. "Fortune seekers don't give a damn about good buns, but Hollywood directors sure do."

Yahoo! We were back on track.

⌁ For the moment, we were maintaining financially. Peter was doing well with orders for wine supplies, and we were making a nice profit even after his expenses, which made me think in the midst of everything else going on that I might be able to do more work from home once I was ready to start back full-time. Peter's leg was healing, too, and we were all pleased about that, yet he showed no signs of being eager to leave us. Peter is, in fact, still on staff. I guess growing up in a family of wine experts, it was expected that he would have certain skills and interests with regard to the wine industry—a good palate, a sense of timing, a fondness for the fieldwork, who knows. But his real talents—his remarkable charisma, his initiative and organizational abilities and his total dedication to problem solving—never got the chance to surface until he came to work for us. Anna and I were so distracted, we never thought to "supervise" Peter. And thank goodness we didn't, because we probably would have been in his way. By the end of his first two months, Peter had redesigned my order/shipping forms so that they actually made sense and were integrated with a computer program that simultaneously issued invoices and billing statements. He'd created an interactive Web site listing all our products and services, and started a newsletter for amateur winemakers. He had opened markets I didn't know existed. I know we wouldn't be where we are, now, without him. By the way, good as he is, he can't tell the difference between a merlot and a chardonnay, let alone the subtleties of vintages. He has no palate. None. Drinks Diet Coke with dinner.

I chatted by phone almost daily with winemakers and billed them for my time. That brought in some income, too. And I slept in my own bed every night. Until that point, I hadn't realized how much I would love having a full-time wife and home. Over the years, the weekly travel had become as much a part of my life as breathing, and I hadn't given much thought to options until now. The initial four weeks I had planned to take off had rolled into two months, and still, everything was running smoothly. Spending week after week with Anna was great. Walking to the post office and the grocery store, having breakfast midweek at the local diner, talking over the fence to our neighbors, being honked at and waved to when I walked into town were all things I had never experienced in my adult life. I liked it. With my consulting income, Peter's magic on the phones and computer and Anna's occasional articles for the local paper, we got by, and I knew I'd never go back on the road full-time again.

But first things first. I thought the news release was a good idea, if only to see what kind of reaction we'd get. The plan was to send it to a few of the big papers around the state. It was truly a shot in the dark, but what Anna and I were pretty much resigned to was that this whole search would be a series of shots in the dark until something clicked. What remained unspoken between us were big *what ifs*. What if we find nothing. What if we're chasing a rabbit down the wrong hole. What if nothing turns up anything. Would the veracity of our efforts be enough to satisfy, pacify Jeanette? Would she . . . could she find enough peace, knowing that we tried, to move on without the proof she had waited ninety years for?

Often I awoke in the night with all this stuff whirling around in my head. We had accepted Roberta's interpretation of the haunting almost without question because we had nothing else to go on. I suppose we could have tried to find another psychic, another medium or channeler—oh great . . . the word isn't even recognized by spell-check. But I'll tell you, this was not like going to another doctor to get a second opinion about a sore back. Roberta had convinced us she knew what she was talking about—or I guess, to be more accurate, that she knew what Jeanette was trying to tell us. And, God knows, the pieces seemed to fit together pretty logically. So we were simply going with our gut, now, to try and find some answers.

One helpful move turned out to be a call that Anna made to a local genealogy society. After we gave them a generic description of the purpose of our search (young baby may have been given up for adoption in 1919, mother and father dead, grandparents raised other sibling . . .), they gave us some tips for locating lost links and showed Anna how to chart our findings. That would prove helpful to keeping our information straight.

The news release employed much the same simply worded description Anna gave to the genealogy society. We included no names, thinking that the new parents would not have known them anyway and that names might simply complicate and confuse the issue, though without them, the release was a bit vague.

Carlston, MI—For immediate release: A couple in this former lumber-mill town are seeking information about an infant who may have been taken from its home in 1919. The baby girl was approximately six months old at the time of her disappearance. Her mother told police that the child was removed from a basket on the front porch in the late afternoon while sleeping. The mother reportedly left the child alone while she checked on a son who was napping in an upstairs bedroom.

According to police reports, the infant could not be located. There were no clues as to its disappearance and no apparent motive for the abduction. The child's mother died a few weeks later.

Recent buyers of the home seek information about this interesting case.

The baby girl was born in early 1919 and was last seen around August 19 of that year. She had dark curly hair and brown eyes. She might have been wearing a sweater with small pearl buttons at the time of her disappearance. All information will be treated with respect and confidentiality. Please write to PO Box 233, Carlston, MI.

That was our final draft. John and I admitted it wasn't much to go on, but it was a start, and we hoped it might be intriguing enough to catch an editor's eye. We sent the release to the Detroit papers, to the *Grand Rapids Press*, the *Traverse City Record Eagle* and a few others. Grace suggested that we pay to send it in the weekly mailing of the Michigan Press Association, and that sounded like a good idea, too. We also turned it into a display ad and ran it for a few weeks in several papers.

Then we waited.

Roberta nearly disappeared from our life. Her café was a busy place and growing, and her competent but young staff needed her around to keep things running smoothly. She was planning to expand into the storefront next door, which would nearly double her space and allow room for the Saturday-afternoon poetry readings and book talks she had dreamed about since opening. She had also scheduled a trio with harp, flute and hammered dulcimer to play during the noon hour. We talked only occasionally. Twice we took a drive to Grand Rapids and surprised her by stopping at the café for lunch.

After those earlier weeks of intense and intimate visits spent trying to figure out what had happened in our house, Roberta was pulling away from us. She was full of hugs and smiles when we saw her, but it was clear that our pursuit of Rose didn't interest her. She was polite but seemed distracted when we tried to talk about our search and the things we were learning. That took us aback. We felt a little abandoned by her, though I knew in my heart that her work with us was nearly finished. She had her own, full life apart from us. She had been a busy woman before we met, and had generously carved out time to help us. She was just going back to the life and the place that were her own. Still, I missed her. Being raised an only child by my grandparents left me loving a house full of people—a noisy, busy place with food cooking on the stove and chatter in the living room and babies crawling around underfoot. Roberta's café gave that kind of feeling. It was always full of people who seemed to know each other, and it smelled good, and there were always children running around. Every time Roberta came to visit, she had brought a bit of that atmosphere with her, and somehow, even though there were only three of us in the house when she was there, it felt like a party. I loved it. And I felt safe. I guess I also thought that as long as Jeanette could communicate with Roberta, she would leave me alone.

It was the end of October by the time we got the release and ads out. Months had gone by since John and I made that first blind foray into Roberta's café. We had a killing frost around the 4th that did in the impatiens and released the tenuous bond between leaf and tree. Our yard was thick with red and gold leaves, which we raked into piles and hauled to the landfill. Such a waste. I longed for the smell of burning leaves that always transported me back to childhood, but the practice had long been declared a dreadful contributor to air pollution and prohibited within the city limits.

It wasn't that I was bored. There was plenty to do. But we were playing the waiting game, and I was not cut out for it.

Halloween came and went. It was fun, as always, but I think I was hoping Jeanette would show up in person, somehow manifest in a physical state and just come knocking. Or that Rose, perhaps still alive, would decide to pay us a visit. Of course, Rose wouldn't likely have a clue that this house was once hers.

I wondered about one of our hypotheses—that she had been taken by religious baby-stealers. And if that had happened, whether she had ever been told the truth. See, when you have the kind of imagination that I have, this is what you spiral to: they told her on her eighteenth birthday, as eighteen seems to be a magic number with parents who have earth-shattering news for their children.

Today, on your birthday (don't mean to squelch your celebration, but . . .), you are old enough to know that you were snatched from your own front porch, stolen from your heathen mother so you could be raised by a good Christian family. You can thank us later.

Good Lord, I wondered, was that possible? Maybe Rose had been back to the old homestead for a visit at some point. Maybe she had only walked around the yard and along the side streets, and did not knock on the door to tell the owners who she was. Surely if she had done that—if she had set foot inside the door, Jeanette would have raised a ruckus to get her attention, moved some furniture or wailed or dropped pictures from the walls. Maybe she would have suddenly become a vapor and wrapped herself like loving arms around her grown-up baby girl. Listen to me. I make this sound like some kind of nearly normal mother-daughter relationship.

↷ *Well, I have to say that anyone stopping by to listen in on conversations* between Anna and me that fall would likely have walked away shaking their heads. Hell, they probably would have run. We spoke of Jeanette as though she occupied a chair at our table—which, in fact, we believed she did. And Rose . . . well, she was like an older sister to us. We talked about where she might have grown up, what her new family was like, whether her parents had encouraged her to go to college. We wondered if she had ever married, and had children. . . . wow. It was possible and probably likely that there were little Rose offsprings who could be in their fifties or sixties now. The possibilities for the trail we might find were exhilarating, until we reminded ourselves that we didn't know anything about Rose, except this: that according to her mother, she had disappeared some ninety years earlier from a basket on her front porch wearing what appeared to be a handmade sweater with three pearl buttons. That was it. The rest . . . well, the rest was pure conjecture on our part. And hope. And in the back of my mind—not so far back actually—was a terrible fear that not finding a trace of Rose meant Jeanette was here to stay. God help us. I had already decided that if we ran into only dead ends, Anna and I would move from Maple Hill and leave Jeanette behind. Much as I wanted to help this woman-spirit who longed for knowledge of her lost child, I wouldn't risk losing Anna again. That decision was not up for debate. And could I sell this house to someone without telling them about Jeanette? Probably. It was even likely that we could get a premium price if we advertised that it was haunted. Some people like that sort of thing.

As the holidays neared, our weekends began to fill with parties, and Anna hauled out our "conveys with the property" collection of Christmas decorations. We had, in fact, negotiated with Margaret to leave behind the miles of garland she had draped over and around everything, and I think she was grateful that she didn't have to take it down herself before she left. She probably knew what we were in for. We began the arduous task of removing it about a week after we moved in, and it was a stinking mess. The stuff outside had been up for years—through rain, snow, sun and several bird-nesting seasons. It had the remnants of a thousand sparrows in it, I swear. We bought those aqua paper face masks to wear for fear we'd inhale some rare virus transmitted by powdery bird droppings, and don't think I didn't worry about that too, when Anna got so sick. Anyway, we scrubbed the garland when we got it down, let it dry out in the yard and packed it away in—what else—wine boxes. And I stashed it up in the rafters of the garage.

When our first Christmas had rolled around, just a couple months after we moved into the house, we were still up to our necks in unpacked boxes, and Anna was already feeling lousy. We had cut a small tree from a local grower, wrapped it in strings of tiny white lights and used our collection of cookie cutters hanging from red ribbons for ornaments. It was easy, and it looked good, and the whole process exhausted Anna. We called it done and didn't put up a single other decoration.

So this year, we said, would be different. We dragged down the boxes of garland and tacked it everywhere—around the pillars on the porch, up the banister, across the tops of doorways and along the edge of the garage roofline. Some of it was pretty easy because lots of the old nails that Margaret had hung it from were still in place. I have to say, it was gorgeous. We entwined most of it with strings of white lights like we used on the Christmas tree that first year, and that made the whole place look like it was glowing at night.

When we finished, two days before Thanksgiving, I stood for about three minutes in ankle-deep fresh snow just staring at our pretty home, thinking about how lucky we were, and how beautiful everything looked, and momentarily I caught Margaret's Christmas fever. I took Anna's hand and suggested we keep the garland up into the summer—that it would brighten dull February and March and give the house a great tropical look in June. She looked horrified and yelled, "My husband is possessed with the spirit of a bad decorator!" She grabbed some snow and threw it at me, then turned and ran toward the house, feigning panic and hollering, "Save me . . . save me!" Just for the record, the garland came down on January 2.

The only phone calls we got were from salespeople or friends—no descendants of long-lost babies, no historian with a closely held dark secret about Carlston. Of course, we hadn't included our phone number in the release, and had instead rented a post office box. I don't know why, exactly. It just seemed like a good idea. It put a little anonymity between us and the rest of the world. We did not include our street address, too, because from that anyone looking could have easily found our phone number. The post office box remained empty, and our house mailbox was full of cards and sales fliers. Nothing more.

⁂ *The day before Thanksgiving, I was digging around in a semi-frozen* turkey, pulling out that little bag of mysterious parts they always put inside for us to throw away, when I heard the dull clunk of our mailbox lid being closed: 12:45. I could practically set my watch by it. In a town this small, there isn't much to disrupt our letter carrier on her short route, and she takes that "Neither rain nor sleet" promise pretty seriously. So, it registered vaguely that the mail had come, and that's the last I thought of it until about 3:30, when I finally sat down with a cup of coffee to check off turkey and green bean casserole from my to-do list.

There must have been a dozen of those glossy little store fliers advertising day-after-Thanksgiving sales, two bills, one Christmas card from friends who always mail theirs around the middle of November. I heard the garage door opening. John was back from the store. He walked in, threw me a weak smile and tossed a couple things on the kitchen table. He had been to the post office and checked our box there.

"Two letters." That was all he said. And he was pale.

I picked up the envelopes. Both were hand-addressed. One was on pink stationery and postmarked from Warren. The other was a plain number-ten business envelope postmarked Flint. John had opened neither, so I slit the plain envelope first, conscious of trying not to get my hopes up.

Dear Sir,
I saw your articale about looking for info about the lost baby. Is there a reward? If yes, call me and I will help you. I have the news you are looking for.

His address and phone were listed below. I know I stared at the paper for several moments, wondering why this guy hadn't cut letters and words out of magazines and pasted them together like a ransom note. His short missive had that same sort of ominous tone, complete with the misspelling. And he had given no name, of course. Of all the weird responses I had braced myself for, this was not one of them. Jeez, a fortune hunter. John, meanwhile, trying very hard not to look interested, had opened a beer and cut himself a slice of cheese.

"Do you want to hear this?" I asked.

"Fire away."

I read it aloud, trying to phonetically pronounce the word "articale." It actually made me laugh a little, and already going through my head was the question of what to do with it. I remembered reading an article about a young writer who, several years earlier, trying to get published for the first time, had moved into a very bare apartment—his first—in New York. Having no money for luxuries like posters or paintings to dress up his plain white walls, he decided to paper them with rejection letters, which became his motivation for continuing to send queries to agents and publishing houses. Eventually, he covered several walls with the turndowns, and, in the process, published several short stories and eventually the first of many novels.

Maybe we were going to be the recipients of a lot of fruitless responses, this being the first, and I thought they might look swell if we glued them to the walls of the bathroom.

John didn't laugh.

"What a shit that guy is."

"Funny that we both think it's from a guy, isn't it?" I asked.

"Anna, how many women do you know who would do this kind of thing?"

I was dumbfounded by his question. I didn't know any women who would do it, but then I didn't know any men who would, either.

His abrupt reaction surprised me, and I told him we couldn't let this get us down. "You know, we opened the door to a lot of opportunistic people out there when we sent that release. If this is as bad as it gets, I'd say we're lucky."

"What a creep."

I decided to drop the idea of papering a wall with it, given John's lack of humor at the moment. I told him I saw no point in answering it because I was sure the guy was a phony. But I did want to save it.

"What on earth for?" John asked. "The guy's a shithead."

That was a sign. John reserved that epithet for the worst of the worst. He was obviously in a snit.

"What's up, honey?"

He started to leave the room and mumbled, "I'm not up for company tomorrow."

I called to him and asked him to come back and talk to me. He turned and stopped, but he said nothing. He just looked at me. He suddenly seemed exhausted, and I knew I needed to tread carefully. John didn't blow up often. In fact, even now, I can't count more than a handful of times he's lost it in my presence. I didn't want that afternoon to be one of them.

"John, is it just because of this letter?"

"No. It's because of this whole damn thing. I don't want people asking us questions about it. I don't want to talk about it. I don't want to think about it. I'm tired. And I'm scared, Anna. What if this is all we get. Phonies. Crap. What if Jeanette isn't satisfied with our efforts. What if she surfaces again? What if I lose you to her again? We have basically nothing to go on and no reason to believe that we'll ever know the truth about Rose. Did that ever occur to you? We have nothing.

Absolutely nothing. And I'm not going to stand here and let some obsessed spirit—who I'm not even sure exists—turn our life upside-down again. I want to move."

John had put down his beer, squared his body to me, punched his hands into his pockets and braced himself in the doorway. He looked like he was ready for a fight.

"Been thinking about this for a while, have you?"

"Only all night. Nearly every night. Anna, I can't even touch you without the creepy feeling that someone is watching us. I can't eat without wondering if Jeanette is tapping her fingers somewhere waiting for us to hurry up so we can get back to the business of finding her damn daughter. It's making me crazy."

"I think you're tired, honey," I told him. It was a little lame, but it was all I could think of. John's mood was rapidly disintegrating, and actually, I figured a nap would do him some good, given his recent string of bad nights. "It's just Karen and Liam and their kids for dinner tomorrow. Nothing big. And it wouldn't be fair to cancel out now. Besides, I have enough food for twenty, so unless you want to be eating green bean casserole for breakfast for the next two weeks . . ."

"I want to move."

"OK, baby." I walked up to John and put my arms around him. He was always so steady. It was hard to see him come unglued. I stood on my toes and brought his head to my shoulder. His hands rested on my waist, and we stood that way, just taking in the stillness of the house, for probably half a minute. His neck was clammy, and he was breathing fast, but he'd gotten out what he needed to say. "I understand that you want to move, John. Let's get through the holidays and talk about it in January."

I took a breath and asked if he was up for opening the other letter. Then I stepped back to look at him and tried to read the answer on his face. Finally, I held up the envelope and slit it open with a knife that had been sitting on the counter. I pulled out a sheet of white stationery and began to read aloud. John could leave the room if he wanted.

My name is Mike Webster. I read your notice in the Detroit Free Press, and I am wondering if perhaps my sister, Mary, could be the child about whom you seek information.

80

The script was easy to read, written by someone who had scored well in penmanship years earlier, a teacher's pride. I reread the first sentence to myself two more times before I dared go on. John had pulled out a chair but didn't manage to actually sit.

"Shall I go on?"

He just stared at me. I took that for a yes.

Mary Webster's birthday was February 14. At least, that is what my parents told us. She turned one in 1920, six months after she came to live with them. She had dark hair and brown eyes like her father, George. And fair skin like her mother, Ella. She grew up in a big house on the outskirts of Detroit and was the oldest of three children. Her sister, Meg, was four years younger. I was their surprise, born two days before Ella's 41st birthday. Mary was already 19. Ella called her children, all of us, her miracle babies.

Mike lived in Tampa, Florida, and had been forwarded a short article from the Detroit paper by his daughter Colleen. She had grown up with her grandmother's stories—and the noticeable gaps—about how her Mary came to live with them, and with Mary's own stories. The description of the baby who disappeared in the same year that Mary was adopted piqued Colleen's interest.

Mike included a few more details about Mary, among them that she grew up lovely and loved. She was a wonderful sister. She married but did not have children. And she preceded her husband, Ed, in death from an aneurism which occurred while she slept, at the age of seventy-one.

There was a phone number and Mike's street and email addresses. While Mary's origins were mostly unknown, he concluded, her hand-carried path to the Websters' was well documented. He encouraged us to call if we thought there was a chance she was the child we were looking for.

My heart was racing, and I wanted to pick up the phone to call Mike immediately. John was less enthralled.

"What if it's a dead end? Are you prepared for that?" he asked with concern.

I answered honestly. "I just want to get started, John. This is a start. No more, but no less. I want to get this resolved. I mean, it's a little late to be second-guessing whether or not we're prepared to do this, isn't it?"

"Can't you wait until Friday or Saturday?"

"Yeah, I can, John, but if you're going to mope around here for the next few days anyway, then I say let's call Mike right now and get it over with. Got anything better to do?"

"Wax my legs?"

I love this man's sense of humor. Perfectly irreverent at exactly the right time.

I dialed and got Mike's answering machine. Then I got cold feet and hung up. Brave, huh? John redialed, and left a message. We were calling regarding Mike's letter about Mary. We'd love . . . like . . . to talk to him further. Feel free to call collect. Our number is blah . . . blah . . . blah. My rock. We poured ourselves some wine, and I think we felt considerably lighter than we had in months. I know we were setting ourselves up for disappointment, but . . . well . . . that was just the way it would have to be.

⁓ *The phone rang about 8:30 that night, and neither of us moved. Then we* both jumped up, stopped, and Anna waved me on. It was Mike, of course, and I wondered if he could hear the anxiety in my simple "Hello." He couldn't know the terrible pressure we felt and didn't have a clue that we were not simply trying to fill another blank line on our family tree. I believed Anna's life was at stake, and while we had crossed the earlier chasm of secrets, I could feel the strain of our search putting notches in what had once been an easy relationship. Just lately, our tempers seemed shorter, and our patience with each other was stretched and without resilience, like an overchewed piece of bubble gum being pulled from the teeth of a six-year-old.

But Mike was a jewel. He loved history and had tried, over the years, after his sister died, to learn more about her birth family. As he grew older and considered the circumstances under which Mary came into the family, he suspected that the stories that had come with her may not have been forthright. And that was why he waited until Mary was gone. His letter to us was just one more in a long parade of letters that he had sent to various people over the years.

It was, to say the least, a crapshoot on his part. Funny, I had never thought that the person responding to our article might also be taking an emotional risk.

After pleasantries, I asked if Anna could get on the extension phone, and if he'd mind if we taped the conversation so we could review the details. Mike thought that was fine. And I took the leap.

"What can you tell us about Mary?"

"Let me start with my mom so the whole story will make sense," he began. "Her name was Ella. When she was twenty-two, she gave birth one terribly cold February morning to twins who were seven weeks early. It's probably routine these days to be able to save little preemies like those two, but then, it was nearly impossible. They lived only a few hours, but it was long enough for my mother to fall grievously in love with them. She named them Elizabeth and Katharine. She had them at home, of course, and a neighbor and midwife helped care for her. According to the midwife, Mother stroked their faces, kissed their hands and feet and told them stories about all the fun they would have playing at Grandpa Webster's farm. She propped herself up in bed and held one tiny bundled infant in each arm until long after dark. She refused to let anyone take them from her. Finally, around midnight, as the story was told to us, exhausted and near collapse, my mother handed her tiny dead daughters to my father, admonishing him to keep them wrapped tightly so they wouldn't get cold, and she was sedated."

"She must have been devastated," Anna responded.

"That she was. And literally inconsolable. She spent several days in bed, wasting away in her private grief while her frantic husband, my poor dad, worried that he might soon lose her, too. It was a visit from my aunt, Mom's sister, Pearl, that changed everything.

"Pearl and Mom often talked about how close they had been growing up—they were just a year apart in age. Their parents, my grandparents Henry and Emma, were hardworking, pragmatic people, second-generation Germans and intellectuals who loved books and the theater and classical music.

"Neither of the girls had spent much of their youth in church, but Pearl's life took a major turn after high school when she decided to marry the son of a Baptist minister. Uncle Walter. They had met at Lake Michigan in June when Pearl and her girlfriends rented a cottage for two weeks to celebrate their graduation. Walter wanted to be a minister, too. That summer, though, he was building houses to earn money for Bible school. He was tall and tan and by all accounts a pretty handsome guy. Aunt Pearl was smitten the moment he walked up to her and said hello.

"They were married in October by Walter's father at his church, which was someplace along the lake. I don't know exactly where. The Websters made the trip all the way across the state for the wedding. It took six hours to get there, and they all stayed at a fancy hotel that they told stories about for years. The day after the wedding, Mom and her parents turned around and drove back home, leaving Pearl to begin her new life with Walter. They were uncomfortable with Walter's parents, who peppered them with questions about the condition of their souls, and they apparently had some misgivings about their new son-in-law. They felt he had a lot of rules. Pearl was also going to be living too far away for their peace of mind.

"I didn't learn that from them. They never said a word to me, and never said anything to Pearl either. But they bent my mother's ear all the way home. Their one consolation was that the new bride seemed happy enough. Being still pretty crazy about each other, according to Mom, they knew the power of love, and they trusted it. And, of course, there was nothing they could do about it, anyway. So, they responded the way smart parents do. They graciously welcomed Walter into the family and grew resigned to seeing their married daughter infrequently after Walter and Pearl settled themselves somewhere in a small town up along the lakeshore.

"Years later, when all the relatives gathered at our house for holiday dinners, I remember Walter's dramatic insistence on saying grace, and his fondness for talking about the wages of sin. Mom used to catch me making faces, and she would wag a finger at me, then wink. I knew she was put off by Walter, too."

I was wondering what all this had to do with Mary, but Mike kept going.

"Pearl and Mom wrote to each other often. Two months after her graduation from high school, Mom married George Webster, my dad, who had been her pal since kindergarten and was her first and only love. George's father gave them a small parcel of land to farm. They built a modest house, and set about the business of growing crops and making a family. The crops did fine. It took Mom five years to get pregnant, and when she thought there was a good chance she was carrying twins, they were overjoyed. There was nothing my mother wanted more than to have babies.

"When Pearl got news that Ella's babies had died, she had Walter take her immediately to the nearest bus station, and she headed east to be with her sister. Aunt Pearl used to tell us about all the strange people on that bus and how she made up stories about them to pass the time. One was an actor, one was a poet, one was a murderer who had escaped from prison. She had a pretty good imagination. When she arrived at the house, she was horrified—that's the word she used to use—at how her sister had deteriorated in just a couple days. She was pale and silent, and in fact, she hadn't made it to the babies' funeral because she was too weak. Dad had stood alone, flanked by his parents and a couple siblings, while the single casket holding the twins was lowered into the ground.

"Pearl stayed two weeks, long enough to get Mom on her feet, and she promised to come back, which she did. Two months later, she showed up with a baby girl who she said had been orphaned by the Spanish influenza. She was tiny and a bit ill—short on background, long on need, according to Pearl. My mother accepted the child without question. The stored-up love that didn't get spent on the twins spilled over in waves for baby Mary—that's what Mother and Dad named her. And that was the first Webster miracle baby."

"Amazing." That was as much as I got out. We were all silent for a few moments.

"Did they ever ask where she came from or how Pearl got ahold of her?"

"Dad didn't ask a lot of questions about anything in life. He took what came his way. My mother was a bit more inquisitive, but she really did believe in miracles, and she never questioned this one. She accepted the child at face value, gave her a name and never looked back. Mary was about five or six when she learned she had been adopted. It didn't bother her, and it made for some wonderful stories. Mary always felt very special—sort of handpicked."

"But didn't anyone else ever ask?"

"Oh, sure. And they got the same story. Pearl said she learned about a couple who died from the flu just a day apart and left a baby. She knew where the baby could have a good home. Period. I know it sounds almost unbelievable, given what's required these days just to cash a check at the local grocery . . . but that's the story we got."

Mike made us laugh. We all knew it was impossible to try to apply today's laws with those being followed—and possibly relaxed—in the middle of a worldwide flu epidemic. And given what John and I had already turned up about the informality of adoptions when young parents were dropping dead right and left, we knew Pearl's story would have been plausible.

"When I got older and started to research our family tree, I got to wondering about Mary," Mike continued. "I've been following up on every lead since, but haven't been able to tie down any more detail about where she came from. I know this is a long shot—you said you thought the child you're looking for was abducted. But this has become a hobby—I'm retired now and have the time to chase stories. And anyway, yours sounded pretty interesting even if it has nothing to do with my sister. So . . . that's my story. Tell me yours."

I had been jotting down the names of all the people Mike talked about to try to keep them straight, and I still had more questions.

"Where did Pearl live?"

"By the time I came along, they were in Grand Rapids. Uncle Walter was called to be minister at a big church there, so they moved in from the lake and lived in the parsonage that the church provided. Before that, I think they were somewhere around Muskegon. Possibly further north. Apparently, they moved a lot. Uncle Walter was a pretty headstrong guy and had an unpleasant habit of upsetting his congregations with his tirades about the fires of hell. Considering that he was only in his twenties when he started in the ministry, I guess his finger-pointing sermons were a bit hard for a lot of the older folks to take. He never mellowed. His visits to us decreased with time, and he wasn't much of a topic around our house, but I did gather that as the years went on, his churches got smaller and his followers were increasingly extreme. He was outspoken to his death about the devil waiting to consume the souls of nonbelievers, and he maintained his lifelong resentment of immigrants and—his word—*foreigners*."

For obvious reasons, John and I had decided in advance not to reveal all we knew about baby Rose. It just didn't make sense to start talking to

86

a stranger about my being possessed—a word we now used with abandon—and we wanted to know more about Mary first. We had been cautioned by genealogy experts not to color someone else's story with our own.

In fact, though Mike thought the connection between Mary and Rose was a long shot, we knew it dovetailed amazingly with one of the possibilities on our list—human intervention disguised as divine instruction. When we got off the phone, John had the same pressing question he had asked months earlier.

"Who would have had the nerve?"

"Women. Maybe the women in Walter's church. They would have had the kind of time on their hands that it took to plan this awful deed. And they probably fed the gossip about Jeanette's heathen ways. I imagine Walter could have done a fine job firing up their sense of mission when he talked about the dire consequences for a child whose soul was not saved."

John got it. "So in the name of God, they stole Rose from her heathen mother and gave her to Pearl's sister? Is that possible? Could people really be so arrogant that they would do something like that?"

I knew it was a leap, but it made as much sense as anything else we had at the moment. And I knew the perpetrators would have felt so righteous.

"Why didn't they take Andre, too?" Anna asked.

"He was too old," I reasoned. He was already talking, and he would have told anybody who cared to listen that he wanted to go home, that he wanted his mama. It would have meant constructing a much more tangled lie."

"So we throw out the fact that Pearl said the baby's parents were killed by the flu?" said Anna. It was more of a statement than a question.

Well . . . there was that. Maybe Pearl got Rose and the story of the dead parents from the people who stole her. Pearl was the wife of a minister, and people would expect her to know the needs of people in the community, and therefore might have believed she would know who could take the baby. They might have even known about her sister Ella's tragic loss. We might never be able to put a name with the hands that actually lifted Rose from her porch cradle, but Mike's sister Mary fit the timetable and most of the profile of our own sketchy story. It was worth checking out.

With Mike in Tampa, there was little prospect of meeting him soon, so we agreed to talk again in a few days, after we pulled together more facts and dates. Of course, we already had every fact we could get our hands on at the time, but we wanted to pause and think this through. We needed a little time to cool off before we headed blindly into what sounded like a very plausible connection.

As it turned out, Mike's was not the only well-written letter we got. People who saw the articles began forwarding our address to others, and to genealogy experts, support groups and private adoption attorneys. In a matter of days, our information leapt to the Internet, and it was open season on us.

I remember a compelling letter from a woman with a story about a girl who had been the illegitimate daughter of a prostitute in her town, and another searching for the siblings of a girl who died at the age of ten after falling off a hay wagon. The circumstances didn't have anything to do with what we knew about Jeanette and what we presumed to know about Rose. But they served to make us aware of how many thousands of people—and that's probably a conservative estimate—want to know the whereabouts of other people.

Before the days when photos of missing children showed up on the sides of milk cartons and postcards, and before there were television programs that invited the parents of missing children to tell their story to a nationwide audience, there were untold numbers of kids and adults who just disappeared. Before DNA testing and dental records, it was very difficult to identify the long-dead and decayed remains of a person discovered in the woods and ravines or buried in a shallow grave in somebody's asparagus field.

We also got ads for Internet-based companies that offered to find anyone anywhere for the remarkably low price of $39.95. And we got no fewer than seven catalogs selling genealogy paraphernalia, including family Bibles, photo albums and engraved gifts for newly found relatives. These subcultures amazed me. I mean, until we started looking for information about a baby that vanished off a front porch, I had no idea that there existed what we came to describe as the lost-and-found-people business. We actually got offers from companies to be distributors of their products, "because you have been through the desperate search for a loved one, you have the sensitivity to understand what others in similar circumstances are going through. You will be able to reach out to them . . ." Blah blah blah. And what would we sell them? How about an engraved headstone for their yard—I kid you not—so that they can "put closure on their tragic loss"?

That was just one of the pitches. John and I were appalled. What kind of creeps will sink so low as to prey on people who are scraping bottom emotionally? We decided to forgo these "unique and extremely lucrative" business opportunities.

There were also responses from hardcore genealogy seekers who sent requests for more information on Rose—not that we had any—along with handwritten, illegible charts that contained nothing that we could decipher, let alone use. I felt like we were tied to all these people by many tenuous umbilical cords, but none belonged to Rose. At times, John and I were overwhelmed just trying to decide what was worth a glance and what we could toss immediately.

One category of letters touched us deeply, and we could pull them out of a day's stack of mail as easily as one pulls a sterling-silver spoon from a pile of stainless. The address was usually handwritten in cursive. The envelope was usually not white, more likely pale yellow, pink or blue. The return address label was the type given to a donor in return for a contribution to a group like the National Wildlife Federation or Habitat for Humanity. The stamp said LOVE or carried the likeness of a famous civil rights leader or dead poet. The look was so consistent we began to laugh a bit over it. And that was good, because there wasn't much that made us laugh these days. Without even discussing it, we felt an obligation to send back notes telling the senders of these sad pastel pleas that their lifelong search for their sister/daughter/mother did not end with us.

We began to think of the letters the same way we viewed the stack of requests that come in the mail at Christmas—give to feed a family of four, give for poor children, give for poor children who need health care, give to help build a house for the homeless, give for medical research, give to save abused horses, give to make the air cleaner and the water purer. In our case these letters were requests to give information to people looking for other people who had disappeared in a myriad of circumstances. While the specifics varied greatly, there was one common denominator—everybody was looking for somebody.

In the end, we did open every single letter we received. It took months, but we sat down nearly every night and read them to each other out loud. There were too many, and they were too scary and odd and full of pain to read silently. With each new letter we became increasingly convinced that Mike held our answer.

We knew there was only a remote chance at best that we would find a source to confirm that his sister Mary was our baby Rose. And frankly, the thought that Jeanette might decide to manifest another unwelcome presence at any time gave a sense of urgency to our search that those who were trying simply to fill in a slot on the family tree couldn't appreciate. We agreed that we wouldn't come to any firm conclusions—nor would we stop our search—until after we had talked more with Mike and nailed down whatever details there were.

～ *Two days before the start of Christmas break in the schools, we got* eighteen inches of snow. The roads were a mess, and to the joy of the students, the schools closed early, announcing they would not reopen until after break. Anna and I decided to give Peter three weeks paid leave. He wanted to head back to Colorado to test his mended leg. The cast had come off a couple weeks earlier, and he was itching to get out. But he assured us he would be back. Peter, rather the lost black sheep in his family's huge wine empire, had found his niche running our comparatively small wine consulting business. He was very good. He had earned every bit of what we were paying him, and was thrilled when we told him we would forward the phones and fax back to our house while he took a well-deserved holiday.

I called Mike on the day of the big snow. It was seventy-eight degrees there, and he was sitting in his backyard beside an orange tree. We talked like we were old friends, exchanging stories about the weather and catching up on the activities of his kids. Mike had three daughters. He'd been married for about ten years when his wife decided she was tired of that life and left. Mike said she had flirted with drugs throughout their courtship and even well into marriage and motherhood. She delicately balanced her maternal responsibilities with her love of antidepressants, and found a way to medicate legally, thus saving the family from finding her dead in a back alley or jailed for buying from undercover cops.

It had been fairly easy for her to explain away her minor indiscretions, the slurred words, the obsessive midnight cleaning frenzies, her occasional emotional meltdowns. It was an act she had learned at her own mother's knee. Mike thought she would outgrow it. But after the divorce, when she was on her own again, she stepped back into habits she'd started in college. In recent years, he's come to the conclusion that a little modern-day medication might have gone a long way to bringing back the woman he fell in love with at sixteen. Bipolar, his therapist had suggested. And out of control. That helped ease his fear that he had somehow driven her away. He was, I gathered, a gifted father who had figured out how to tell his daughters about sex and boys, put all three girls through college and watched them bloom into a chemist, a horse trainer and a writer. It was the chemist, Colleen, who had seen the article about our search and sent it to him.

At some point, when I mentioned we were suffering with the blizzard of the century, he laughed and suggested we come visit him.

"I have three bedrooms, one small fishing boat and the best view of the bay that a retired historian can buy," he had joked. "Really, hop a plane, and come down. Family should be together at the holidays, and it feels like we're practically family."

In truth, I thought Anna was the ultimate bonder with strangers, but Mike was yards ahead. There never was a barrier with him, despite the risks we were all taking by exposing our tender, unfinished stories.

Mike's daughters and their families were in various places around the country, and each would be coming in to visit for a few days, but at least one bedroom, he assured us, would be available throughout the holidays. And, he cracked, if it got too crowded, there were always the hammocks on the lanai, which he thought might be the best place to sleep anyway.

Thinking his offer was just polite, and that the possibility of us going to Tampa was remote, I told Mike we would pack up some photos of Rose and her family and ship them to him so he could compare them with the photos he had and see if there was any resemblance.

I finished the conversation and hung up the phone feeling pleased and happy and the most settled I could remember in months, only to find Anna staring at me with her hands on her hips and a big smile on her face.

"So, when do we leave?"

❧ *John looked startled by my question. In fact, he didn't just look it: he WAS* startled.

91

"Funny girl."

"John, I can't believe you didn't jump on this. What about an invitation to spend the holidays in Florida with a new friend do you find so easy to turn down? Why on earth are we staying in Michigan for Christmas? We have no family nearby, and no big plans for the holidays. Getting out of town sounds like a swell idea. Why not Tampa? And isn't this what we were hoping for? A face-to-face with the guy who may have our answers? And a face-to-face someplace where it's eighty degrees instead of twenty? And what about . . ."

Well, I don't remember exactly what I said, but you see, this is my style. I pounded John with questions and didn't give him time to answer any of them, and finally, I just wore him down. Nasty habit I have. As it turned out, we weren't the only ones trying to get out of the snow. The flights were full, and compounding that little dilemma was the effect of the storm on the airlines. It caused so many cancellations throughout the Midwest that it took a couple days to get stranded families cleared out of the airports and on to their final destinations. After much checking, we decided to celebrate Christmas at home and head to Florida on the 26th. John had a huge bank of frequent flier miles, but all the award seats were taken. For the first time in years, we paid full fare. As for the business from which we'd released Peter for three weeks, John decided a well-phrased message on the answering machine would let folks know we'd be back in a week to take their calls. We'd bring the laptop and could check email daily from Florida. When we called Mike back to ask if he was serious about the invitation, he said yes and insisted we stay with him. I wagered that the high cost of the airfare was balanced by our not having to spend anything for lodging. For a week. And if Mike got tired of us, or if he turned out to be creepy, or if the house had rats, well . . . there were always the hammocks he mentioned, or we could just come back home.

Five

⤳ *I have an older sister we haven't told you about yet. Janice flipped out in* high school and headed to San Francisco when she was seventeen. My folks were horrified, of course, and had conveniently ignored all the warning signs pointing to the fact that she was a troubled kid ready to explode. They spent thousands of dollars trying to find her, with no success. About six months after her disappearance, they got a postcard with a couple sentences and a postmark from California, so at least they knew she was alive and probably reasonably coherent. They stopped wringing their hands and pretty much stopped talking about her after a while. They had lived through the worst of the embarrassment of being the only parents they knew who had a kid who went bad. At least now they could tell everybody that their darling daughter was in Northern California, living the life of a Bohemian poet. They tried to make it sound exotic, and after a couple weeks, friends kindly stopped asking for details.

Janice just sort of floated out of our lives. I knew her birthday was a really tough day for my mom. Christmas was actually not so bad as most of my folks' friends had kids away at school or working someplace halfway around the world. They were all feeling abandoned by various offspring to some degree, and it made for a lot of camaraderie.

There were, for years, always a couple extra gifts under Mom and Dad's Christmas tree, "in case Janice makes it home this year." *Makes it home* . . . I loved that. . . . they made it seem like she might call at any moment and blithely announce that she had been given a bonus and some extra vacation days and was hopping on the next plane so she could spend the holidays with her beloved family.

When I was young, the whole scene made me mad. I was OK being the only child in the house at that point, but with the ghost of Janice always hovering, I felt I was competing with shadows for my parents' affection. The unclaimed Christmas presents disappeared when the tree came down. I wasn't brave enough to ask Mom what she did with them. I also never found out what was in those boxes, and believe me, I spent a lot of time wondering what Mom thought would be an appropriate gift for a runaway girl.

At any rate, you get the picture. There was a lot of pain in my house. If you have children, perhaps you can imagine what it's like to have your only daughter turn her back on you and walk out of your life. In a rare, candid moment, Mom told me that some days she wished a telegram would come notifying her that Janice was dead so she could stop worrying about her.

One afternoon, about ten years after she split, Janice showed up on my parents' doorstep. They barely recognized her—she was a mess. As far as they could tell, she'd been living on the streets much of the time and was greatly in need of a bath and a bed at a rehab center. Mom made a huge deal about seeing her . . . really huge. I can only imagine the scene, with all their enthusiasm and their iterations of how worried they had been. And then, of course, there were their millions of questions.

Janice lasted one hour. When she excused herself to use the bathroom, she walked in, shut the door, opened the window, pushed out the screen and vanished. Mom went to check on her after about ten minutes. Dad heard Mom scream, and he knew immediately that they had overwhelmed their fragile daughter and driven her away. Again.

I was out of college by then and living in Albany. When Janice first showed up that day, Mom and Dad had insisted on calling me immediately so she could talk to me, too. I was not home, so they left a jubilant message on the recorder, then passed the phone to an unenthusiastic Janice. She said, "Hello, John. I'm here with Mommy and Dad." *Mommy?* She sounded old and tired and so different from the sister I'd known, that I thought she might be an imposter.

94

The next message was from my anguished mother.

"She's gone again. Oh, God, John. Gone again. Call us, honey. Please."

Then I could hear my father, who was apparently standing next to her, and I heard him trying to console her and tell her to hang up the phone. They were wrecked.

I vowed right then, listening to my mother sobbing, that if I ever found Janice, I would simply kill her.

I hated her so much at that moment. She had overshadowed my own childhood when she left the first time. And I hated her for giving my parents false hope and leaving them even more devastated now, more desolate than they had been ten years earlier. It was unbelievably cruel.

So, where does this all fit in?

Years later, I got a note from her. She was in Tampa. Small world. She said she had gotten clean after spending a few months in a county-run drug center, following her arrest for soliciting an undercover cop. She was working as a waitress at a seafood house. And she wanted to know how Mom and Dad were. She had gotten my address from an old high school friend of hers whom she had stayed in touch with over the years who suggested she call the high school office to see if they had an address for me. I, having loved nearly every minute of high school, had been to every reunion and updated my information for the alumni directory every time I moved.

I fired back a letter to Janice.

Mom and Dad were old, I told her. Much older than the actual years they had both logged. They were nearly overcome with guilt and suffering from all sorts of things that are brought on by the deadly combination of stress, depression, regret, rejection and parenthood gone awry.

I told her she was an ungrateful bitch, a demonic whore who ruined everything she touched. And I told her I'd kill her myself if I ever saw her again. She didn't write back.

John never talked about Janice. In fact, in the years we'd been together, I think we had exactly one lengthy conversation about her—not with her, just about her. I knew exactly how John felt about her, and I saw no reason to try and change his mind. But now that we were going to

95

Tampa, it occurred to me that John might consider trying to contact his wayward sister. He had mellowed somewhat, and had been through a good bit of therapy trying to understand the dysfunction in his family. Janice was really the tip of the iceberg, to be trite. John's father was a mouse, and his grandfather was a world-class philanderer. His mother struggled with violent depression, which became more pronounced after the death of her third child, a girl who succumbed to complications of pneumonia when she was four months old.

I think being in love made John want to talk to somebody to figure out what demons, if any, he had stored inside. I was really glad for that, though I didn't make a big deal out of it. But all you had to do was sit back and listen to the weird stories about the people who surrounded him as a child. It wasn't much of a leap to think that someday he'd have some big baggage to wade through.

John came out of therapy with compassion for his sister and an understanding of his misplaced youthful anger toward her. He saw his parents a little more clearly, which led to understanding his own fears and mood swings. And perhaps most important, he put the ugly stuff mostly behind him and moved on. So as you might guess, I had no idea what he would do about Janice. We didn't even know if she was still in Tampa.

~ *I hadn't spent a lot of time in Florida, as you can imagine. It's not exactly* a popular spot for wineries, and because I travel so much for my wine work, if a place isn't populated with wineries, I probably haven't been there lately. Places like New Mexico and Arizona are still on my "to see" list. Last time I was in Florida, I was about seven. My parents took us there one March when Dad was laid off from his job as an accountant for a construction company for a few months. We stayed with my grandparents, who had made their annual trek to sleepy Pompano Beach in October and were comfortably settled in a little rented house about a block from the ocean. It was a fun place for a kid. The neighborhood was safe then—safe enough for me to be allowed to wander by myself to the beach to hunt for shells and poke at the helpless jellyfish washed ashore at high tide until I was called home for supper.

Tampa, several decades after my Pompano Beach adventures, was, by contrast, a big city with holiday traffic, canyons of hotels and condominiums, a few murders and fabulous food. But I need to back up a bit. We arrived at the airport at four p.m., rented a car and followed the directions Mike had given us to get to his house. Since he'd been a historian all his adult life, it shouldn't have surprised us that he lived in a turn-of-the-century Spanish-style bungalow in a neighborhood of other old homes, most in various stages of renovation. Mike had bought the house when he retired and was working on it room by room, patching old stucco, replacing iron balconies and trying to stay one step ahead of the little salamanders that crept in through cracks in the foundation, and occasionally sauntered boldly right through the French doors. It was a treasure. Our bedroom window was draped outside with bougainvillea, and just beyond it was a small grove of ancient orange trees.

Our first dinner with Mike and his daughter Colleen was relaxed and easy. I don't think it was our possible common bond that made the evening so pleasant. It's just Mike. He's every bit as nice in person as we found him to be on the phone.

Having never been in Florida at Christmas, I was fascinated by the sight of colored lights strung in palm trees. But truly, the giant blow-up Santas and snowmen, dressed in their plastic winter coats and hats and anchored on people's front lawns next to fruiting orange trees, were the funniest, most out-of-place-looking things I'd ever seen. I figured the owners were probably transplants from the North who had simply brought their snowy-weather Christmas decorations with them and hadn't yet redressed their Santas for the tropics.

Not so, Mike assured me.

"Santa puts on heavy clothes when he hops on the sleigh at the North Pole, and he finishes his delivery of toys around the world so quickly that he doesn't have time to change his attire when he arrives in balmy Florida."

Mike wasn't exaggerating when he told us he was a good cook. Anna, reminding me it was Christmas, had shopped for dried cherries and Michigan-made chocolates before we left Carlston. Then she added a few jars of her homemade jams and packed it all in popcorn so we could ship it through as baggage. Mike was delighted with her choices and immediately added a handful of the cherries to the salad he was making for dinner. For my part, I had filled a wine shipper with twelve bottles of our favorites, including, of course, Chateau Nevermore. That, too, was checked as luggage.

Mike picked out a bottle of a sturdy cab, and by the time the four of us sat down to eat, we were like chummy old friends. Colleen, who mirrors her father's grace with strangers, and who was responsible for our meeting in the first place, had plans that night with friends and left before dessert. Anna and I were sorry to see her go, but she is not a student of history like her father. Being young, she was looking forward to a night of dancing at a local club, not sitting around with old farts discussing the details of a possible kidnapping that happened decades before she was born. In fact, it wasn't until the three of us finished the last of a yule log Mike had made for Christmas that Anna brought up the topic and we remembered we were there to try to put together the pieces of a puzzle.

"Did Mary ever talk about her first life?" Anna began. "I know she was too young to remember anything, but did she seem interested in finding out where she came from?"

"She never asked about it," Mike replied. "And I never would have guessed that she cared or even thought about it, except that I came across a poem she wrote. She was still single and had moved into an old house while she went to college. Apparently she was taking a poetry class, and the house inspired some creativity."

Mike had found the poem in a box of Mary's papers in the attic of their parents' house. He went to the kitchen, brought back a box of things he'd put aside for us to look through and pulled out the small, slightly tattered sheet of white paper. Mary had dated it February 2, 1939. It had no title. Mike read it to us.

This house is mine now.
And I know little about it but this
There was at least one baby rocked by her papa in a hand-made cradle in the
*   tiny bedroom at the top of the stairs.*
And there was one young mother, unprepared for this tiny miniature of herself,
Who died giving birth.
This old house yields few tales
But this one is out,
Given over on brittle newsprint,
Stuck in a Bible that slipped unnoticed behind the radiator.

It was a tender touchpoint. Maybe Mary had given more thought to her birth parents than she let on.

I was moved by the sweetness of the poem and by its sadness. Actually, when Mike finished reading it, I could barely breathe. If it was true that Mary was our baby Rose, this was the first tangible evidence we had of her. I reached out to touch the paper, and I held it like it was an original of the Declaration of Independence. That's sort of ironic as I think back on it, because if we did find in Mary the answers that Jeanette sought for more than ninety years, that would certainly result in independence from our resident spirit.

I was terribly envious of Mike for having known Mary for so many years. Had we moved to Maple Hill sooner, perhaps we would have begun our search earlier and would have been able to meet Mary while she was still living. I wanted to know everything—how she looked, what she liked, how she did in school. And somewhere during that first long night of talking, I had the overwhelming feeling that we might be a little too late to put the pieces together.

At about two a.m., Anna suggested we go to bed, and that was wise. I was starting to get philosophical—something that was very easy with Mike, because he was so happy asking questions and just sitting back to hear the answers. He pulled stuff out of me that I hadn't thought about in decades . . . and about the time I was ready to open a new bottle of wine and get really maudlin, Anna stood up and extended her hand to me. It was her sign to me that she was ready to retire and that probably I should be too.

Colleen headed back home the next day, and I offered to cook supper while Mike shuttled her to the airport. During my first trip to the local grocery, I had discovered all kinds of wonderful cheeses, breads, olives, locally grown fruit and other treasures you have access to when you live in a city with more than twenty-five hundred people. Anna had gone for a walk. When Mike came home, he pulled up a chair in the kitchen so we could talk while I made dinner.

"So is the big question here whether or not we think my aunt and uncle kidnapped Rose?" he asked. "Is that what this boils down to?"

"I don't know, Mike," I said. And I really didn't. Honestly, I thought there could be so many possibilities in this riddle, and now that we were away from our house—the scene of the crime—a part of me was quite willing to leave that whole complicated mess behind.

"Anna thinks maybe somebody else took Rose and then gave her to

Pearl, complete with the story about her parents both dying of the flu," I responded.

"That certainly sounds possible, too." Mike, I could tell, was struggling with the thought that Pearl was a kidnapper. By the time he came along, Aunt Pearl was nearly twenty years older than when she had presented a supposedly orphaned baby to her grieving sister. From all the stories his mother told, he knew Pearl had been worn down over time. Assuming she had shared Walter's religious convictions in the early years of their marriage, and that she was as devoted to him as Ella believed, Mike reluctantly suggested that it would have taken little convincing from Pearl's dominant husband to imbue the young woman with the boldness to "rescue" a baby headed for hell.

Anna is right. *Proof* is a funny word. It's a term bakers use for the process of putting yeast breads to rest and rise from their heavy, elastic, globby state to fragrant, airy and doubled in size. It's what county courts need a little of to convict someone of minor theft, and what federal juries need a lot of to assume guilt.

And what on earth did the philosopher mean by "the proof is in the pudding"? Did he see faces of the guilty in that thin, rubbery skin that forms on top? Would Jeanette write "thank you" in our vanilla custard?

Anna and I had never used the word *proof*. Not at home when we searched through acres of mail, not at Mike's house when we tried to fit our few glimpses of Rose's life into the bigger picture of Mary's. But of course, we both knew that proof was what we had come for. And by the end of the week, we were pretty sure . . . actually, we were more sure than that . . . we were *very* sure that we were as close to proof as we were going to get. Our puzzle still had a few holes, but unlike our first steps at putting the story together in the fall, when it seemed there were 499 pieces missing and we didn't have the box cover to guide us, this puzzle had people and houses and roads and trees.

There were questions that remained. We had come to believe Pearl knew more than she ever revealed about Mary's origins, though she never changed her story. And it seems the family made it easy for her to hold fast to the original version. Once "Mary" was placed in Ella's arms, it is clear that there ceased to be any questions about her past until Mike decided to take a closer look many decades later.

The stories that were passed down about Mary coming to live with her new parents were all about the astonished look on Ella's face, the way she took to Mary instantly—and Mary to her—and the fact that everyone pretty much believed Pearl saved Ella's life. ("Sister Ella put on four or five pounds in as many days!") Beyond the brief explanation that the baby's mother and father had both died from the flu within hours of each other, which was completely possible during that time, there was no talk of birth parents. The small matter of legal documentation was managed with the aid of a sympathetic county clerk who accepted the condition of Mary's parents as anonymous and deceased, and processed a certificate of adoption by Ella and George. He was, according to Ella's version of the story, buried in paperwork and the recording of hundreds of death certificates, and he was not looking so well himself.

We had not pinned down exactly where along the lakeshore Pearl and Walter were living when Rose disappeared. Mike had only a small collection of family papers. Most anything having to do with Walter, including boxes of torturous sermons, had been burned in the days following his death. We had to be content with a general description of "along the lakeshore." Pearl and Walter, incidentally, never had children.

Mike told us he had heard Ella occasionally slip in the presence of her children and refer to her brother-in-law as Crabby Uncle Walter. She had no use for the way he shook his finger at her miracle children, and absolutely no tolerance for his gruff, lecturing ways with all of them. He apparently lived his own hell on earth, plagued by visions of heathens perishing in the fires for having turned away from the Word. He lamented the scourges he believed were savagely consuming souls—birth control, liquor and adultery—the last being the inevitable result of liberal use of the first two.

When she was in her early forties, Mike told us, Pearl showed up at Ella's door one cold spring morning with the shadow of a bruise over her eye, and everyone assumed, without asking, that Pearl would leave Uncle Walter. She stayed with Ella's family for five days, until Walter, contrite and uncharacteristically quiet, paid her a visit, packed her suitcase and took her home. The incident was never mentioned, but Pearl's weekly letters to Ella stopped. Ella struggled over what to do and how to help Pearl. She was afraid that making an issue of Walter's behavior would result in his forcing even greater distance between the sisters, which Ella could not bear. It was best, she felt, to continue writing, continue calling when she knew Walter would be at work, and to keep the door open, literally and figuratively.

Walter made noises like he knew God pretty well, but God apparently had secret plans for Walter. Pearl happily accepted Ella's invitation to move in with her sister's gentle family after Walter dropped dead of a heart attack in his early fifties.

A recurrent theme of Walter's sermons had been God's promise to provide, which, you might guess, led to the inevitable discovery after his death that the pastor had no life insurance and nothing so practical as a savings account. Walter and Pearl had lived in parsonages early on, when Walter's churches were large and well funded, and in rented houses in later years when the churches were small and poor. Walter had waved away offers of pension plans over the years, not wishing to appear as though he didn't trust the Divine's intentions. I found that funny. Maybe God's way of providing included a church retirement fund. Whatever. The result was that Pearl was left with very little money in their checking account after Walter's funeral expenses, and there was enough for about one month's bills in, I swear, the cookie jar.

What Pearl did not know about, however, was a small savings account that had been started for her by her parents shortly after she married. Certain that any inheritance passed onto Pearl would be immediately squandered on the church-of-the-week by Walter, her farsighted parents had made Ella trustee of her sister's account. When the girls' mother died two years after their father, Ella divided her parents' assets according to their written wishes, which included depositing a portion into Pearl's secret account.

About a week after his mother-in-law died, Walter had called to inquire about disposition of the will. Mike remembers his father taking the phone call. Calmly, he explained that the will specified that 80 percent of the assets be divided among a Buddhist monastery in Arizona, an animal rescue league in Detroit and a free health clinic for migrant workers in South Texas. The remaining 20 percent was to be sent to an organization through which they had sponsored a family for years in Sierra Leone.

"There wasn't much to pass on anyway," Mike had added. "The girls' parents had been spending down their savings for several years by sending large checks every Christmas to their favorite charities serving the needs of migrant farmworkers and the poor along the Texas-Mexico border."

Walter must have gone white. He had no use for Henry and Emma when they were alive, and apparently believed his heathen in-laws were completely capable of giving everything away to fellow heathens and misguided liberals. The subject never came up again.

The children, who adored their grandparents and thought them eccentric and wonderful, didn't doubt for a moment the truth of their father's explanation. And part of what he said was true. There wasn't much money for Ella and Pearl to split, but only because the will specified that a significant amount of whatever remained be established as trust funds for the three grandchildren for their college educations. It wasn't until Pearl moved in with the Websters and Ella presented her with the passbook for the account started by her parents so many years before that the story came to light.

Mike told us that Pearl's final days were happy ones, but it was clear that she had paid big for her devotion to Walter. She was weary and friendless, thanks to Walter's desire to find abundant sin in everyone Pearl brought home. He had the charming habit of pointing out exactly what God disapproved of—and the requisite punishment—on first meeting. It was a behavior he actually cultivated, fine-tuned even, as he felt dispensing this information was his obligation, rather like one might tell a friend who has a piece of spinach stuck on a tooth or toilet paper stuck to a heel.

Ella knew that Christmas had always been Pearl's saddest day of the year. She had no kids, no friends and a husband who hurled accusations of blasphemy at shopkeepers who put Santa and snowmen in their windows. Christmas dinner was shared in their home with Walter's selection of four or five couples from his current church whom he considered to be the most pious and worthy of his hospitality. The day, Pearl confided to Ella, was always an unbearable combination of discussions of the book of Revelation and modest celebration constrained by Walter's fervor.

Even after decades of interest and with the addition from her parents' estate, Pearl's account wasn't very big, but it was enough for her to suddenly realize she could do something she had always dreamed of—she could be generous. She had not driven in twenty years, so she gave Walter's car to the Websters and asked Ella to take her shopping.

She bought gifts for everyone, including a down comforter for George and Ella, picked out the thickest Christmas tree she could find and had it delivered to the house, then walked downtown arm-in-arm with her sister to admire the animated Christmas decorations in the shop windows.

Christmas day started early and ended late, and Pearl apparently never stopped smiling. She giggled at her first taste of eggnog, and indulged in her newly discovered fondness for chocolate creams. Mary, with whom Pearl had maintained a special closeness, was living with her husband in Fruitport, and the two surprised the family by arriving in time for breakfast. Mike said he had never seen a Christmas tree so beautiful and piled so high with gifts. It took them three hours to open everything.

Two nights later, on December 27, Aunt Pearl died in her sleep. She had not been ill. The autopsy revealed that like Walter, she'd had a heart attack. The children used to say she died of an attack of heart.

After Pearl's estate was settled, miscellaneous papers and boxes of Walter's sermons and diatribes were taken to the back forty to fuel a substantial bonfire. The only significant things kept were marriage and death certificates, which Mike had shown us. If we felt we needed to know where Pearl and Walter lived at the time of Rose's disappearance, we could start checking tax records at the county seats up along the lakeshore, and probably also ask to see local church membership records. Searching for information about long-dead relatives has become a pretty popular pastime, and our requests would not have been considered unreasonable, nor probably rare.

John was dozing on the lanai when a story in the newspaper caught my eye. It was about a Nazi "breeding program" designed to produce children with the blue-eyed, blond-haired Aryan traits that Hitler idealized. Nearly forty adults known as Lebensborn Kinder, or "source of life" kids, had discovered their role in the plan and were meeting to support each other and to share details of their lives. Of the estimated five thousand to eight thousand children born into Lebensborn homes in Germany, some were raised by their birth mothers, but many were given to families of high-ranking SS officers to be raised according to Nazi doctrine.

It was hard for me to think about Pearl doing something as heinous as abducting a baby in the name of giving it to a more deserving mother. Yet, reading the article about the Nazis, who had apparently done it openly and in great numbers, gave some credence to our theory of the connection between Pearl and Rose. I began to think of Pearl as someone sweet, meek and malleable, whose concerns for Rose were likely fanned by Walter's fanatic bigotry. Perhaps she was well-intentioned, just disastrously ill-advised.

There was another story in the paper that day. "Mild-mannered wife of preacher snaps after years of physical and mental abuse and fills her husband with buckshot."

Six

   It has been left to me to me to bring you up to date on Janice. Or at least to get the story started. John's pretty tired of it, but he'll kick in here shortly with the details. He did, of course, decide to try to find his sister while we were in Tampa. Despite his anger, he had developed a lot of compassion for her in the past few years. She had made some very bad decisions at a time in her life when they cost her dearly, and as far as we could tell, she had been paying interest on the mistakes all her adult life. We didn't wonder why she had problems, because, as we told you, pretty much everybody in his immediate family was troubled in a big way. They all could have benefited from some therapy. But we did wonder what fates spared John the addictive personality Janice struggled with, and why Janice's teenage experimentation with drugs morphed into full-scale, decades-long abuse, while John's paved the way for a lucrative career and well-developed self-control.

John had read enough about addiction over the years to know that the odds for Janice's recovery were not in her favor. That bothered him on several levels. He certainly wanted to see his sister clean, and I think in the back of his mind, he wanted the kind of holidays where family members fly in from all over the country and stay for days and everybody gets along and has a wonderful time. But there was something even bigger that he struggled with. There wasn't much that John didn't think he could fix, given enough information and half a roll of duct tape. The fact that he might not be able to fix his sister . . . well, I'm not sure he was willing to accept that. Of course, there was always the chance that she was one of those rare individuals who makes it out of rehab and goes on to create a new life.

Four days into our visit with Mike, I came home from a walk on the beach to find John bent over the local phone book. She was listed. Janice Hillard. It was that simple. He picked up the key to the rental car and told me he was going for a drive. Then he stopped at the door and asked if I would come with him. I knew he was headed to Janice's house, so I nodded and followed. I wasn't going to miss meeting the sister-in-law from hell.

On the way to the car, we took a detour to the backyard, where Mike was pruning a grapefruit tree. The evening before, John had mentioned to Mike that he had a long-estranged sister who, last he knew, lived in Tampa. Mike, ever the skilled researcher, had extracted enough of the story from John to get a good picture of Janice in the past tense and a healthy respect for the unknown Janice in the present tense.

"We're going to try to find Janice," John told him now.

"Janice is a lucky girl to have you for a brother," Mike said quietly. Having watched his wife crash and burn, it's likely Mike knew far better than we what we could be in for.

John said he felt he owed Janice an apology for his ugly letter years earlier and for turning his back on her.

Mike had looked at me with an intensity I had not seen in him before. He began peeling off his well-worn garden gloves—a move so natural to him that I don't think he even knew he was doing it. I stared at the gloves, which were the color of caramel and so clearly used to being on Mike's hands that the soft creases in the leather across the knuckles and palms matched his own.

"John, you did your best, and so did Janice," he said, squaring himself to me. "Sometimes our best doesn't feel like it measures up when we look back at it years later, but at the time you did what you felt you had to do. You both can start out with a clean slate now. Don't look back, my friend. It seldom helps." He smiled a little and sighed. Mike didn't seem like a guy who was accustomed to giving advice, but I believe he had been thinking about this since our discussion the night before. I appreciated his words. He also said he was cooking that night and that supper would be waiting for us if we came home hungry.

Home. What a great word. I remember looking at Mike and realizing that Anna and I had made ourselves a new pal. Mike had created a sense of peace and balance in his life that I have seen in few others—shaped by success and mistakes, refocused by tragedy, matured by perspective. Mike was easily one of the nicest people I had ever encountered. And that Anna and I were staying in his house and feeling like two of his well-loved kids was by far my best Christmas present that year.

"Take care, John. I hope it goes well."

"Thanks. Me too," I replied.

Mike put on his gloves and turned back to the grapefruit tree.

"By the way," he said to us over his shoulder, "I'm making enough food for a small village, so there will be plenty if you find anybody interesting you want to bring home."

Home. There it was again. Mike never said *my home.* Not even *my house* or *the house.* It was *home.* As much ours as his. I started laughing and yelled back a thank you, then looked at my watch. It was 3:30.

With Anna by my side in the rental car, I navigated the streets of Tampa and headed for Janice's neighborhood. It was a beautiful sunny day, and the plastic blow-up lawn Santas were wafting in the tropical winds. The neighborhood was creepy, but I wanted to reserve judgment until I was face-to-face with my sister. When I realized that the house numbers were going up a lot faster than I was ready for, and that Janice's house was probably within spitting distance, I must have made a noise—some kind of snort or gasp. Anna turned and looked at me, but didn't say anything. I was beginning to regret inviting her along, only because I was embarrassed by the fact that I was uncharacteristically losing it. I kept trying to tell myself I was doing this for my parents. That was bullshit, of course. I told Anna that I thought we should have called first.

"Why don't we just drive by, John? It won't hurt to take a look. If you feel like stopping in, we can do that. We can go find a pay phone and call her first."

Anna . . . always the practical one. She was right. We weren't committed to anything just yet, except finding a phone if we decided to call Janice. Did I mention that Anna and I are possibly the only adults in North America who don't have cell phones? This was one of the few times I regretted that.

I was suddenly not even sure what I'd say to this woman with whom my last communication was a death threat. For years, in my mind, I had lectured her about my stolen childhood and the way she had pissed away her life on drugs and booze. But now that I might actually see her, I half wanted her to come running out of her pastel stucco house, straight into her baby brother's arms, and gush Merry Christmas wishes. I wanted our roller-coaster childhood to be replaced with something that felt good. I wanted a memory of a family that had happy times. I wanted us to look like those kids on the covers of the *Saturday Evening Post* that Norman Rockwell had painted—kids with peachy skin and silly smiles, with a frog or a kitten stuck in the pocket of their overalls and a dog who followed them everywhere, contented kids who slept under a patchwork quilt made by an apple-doll-faced grandma somewhere. I wanted my parents to be the parents he painted, too—the confident ones who smiled a lot and looked like they loved their kids and did fun things like dress in Santa suits and hide Easter eggs and make Halloween costumes. Listen to me. I guess three years of therapy can only take you so far, eh? Well, at least I knew what I wanted. And I knew where my pain had come from. If we couldn't change the past, maybe Janice and I could just start from here and at least stay in touch.

"Maybe everything will be OK, and Janice and I can start a new chapter." I was suddenly thinking out loud.

"Well, honey, it looks like you might get that chance. This is her house, and there's a car in the driveway."

I drove past it, and went two more blocks to a liquor store on the corner and parked.

"John?"

We had been sitting there in silence for a few minutes. Just sitting. I hadn't said a word since I pulled up to the curb, and I guess Anna was wondering whether we were going to grow old there.

"Anna, is this stupid?"

"Nope, it's not. But it's also not mandatory. You've lived for years without Janice in your life, and you've done fine. I suspect if you drive away now, you may spend a little time wondering what if, but you will be OK and life will go on."

"Yeah. I guess I don't know what I'm trying to do by seeing her."

"You want my opinion?" She had turned toward me and rested both her hands on my arm. She looked at me with that wonderful honest face and then leaned close and kissed my cheek. "I think you're curious, and you want everything to be all right. And if it's not all right, you're going to want to try to fix it. That's the way you are, John."

I was getting sweaty, even though the car was still running and the air-conditioner was on. Anna nodded her head and smiled. "You can do this."

She knows me well. I walked into the liquor store, and by the way, wouldn't you think I might have had some kind of omen given the proximity of this seedy store to Janice's house? I pulled out the piece of paper from my pocket that had her number on it and asked the tattooed kid behind the counter if he had a phone I could borrow.

He raised an arm and gestured toward the side of the building.

"Outside," he said, and went back to his cell phone conversation and the comic book he was looking at when I rudely interrupted him.

The problem with building a picture of the person you haven't seen in years is that we tend to focus on the fantasy, which can never be as good as the reality. Janice and I just needed to talk. That was where we would start. And with Anna there to help fill the gaps in our conversation, I knew we would be OK.

There was a moderately gross pay phone semi-attached to the wall outside, but given that there are hardly any pay phones around anymore, I was grateful. I dialed.

She answered.

"Hi, Janice, it's John." There was no reaction. "Your brother."

I heard her breathing.

"Janice, is this you?" This was going to be harder than I thought.

"John?"

"Yeah, it's me, Janice. I'm here in Tampa." Down the street at a creepy pay phone that I cannot bear to put up next to my ear because the handset is warm and sticky, and there's a used condom dangling from the hook where the phone book used to be. "I wondered if I could stop by. Actually, I'm here with my wife, Anna. I don't think you've met." I know damn well you haven't met.

"It's been a long time, John."

"Yeah, I know it has. I know the last thing you heard from me was pretty unkind. I was young and angry, Janice, and I'm sorry. Do you have any interest in getting together for coffee or something? I'd really like to see you if you have time."

I was remembering that last "demonic whore" correspondence I'd sent her so many years ago, and suddenly, I couldn't think of any good reason that Janice would have for wanting to see me. None. She had been an addict who couldn't control her impulses. I knew she was not responsible for the things she had done. But I was her brother, in full control of my faculties. I should have been compassionate and understanding. Instead, I had been unforgivably cruel.

"Where are you right now?" Janice sounded guarded, but there was something else I heard in that simple question. Maybe a smile?

OK. Do I lie? No. Better to start out with the truth.

"I'm just down the street. We located your house and saw a car in the driveway and decided to call and see if you were up for some company." Oh crap. Did that sound weak? I'm making it seem like we were just passing by on our way to the grocery store.

"You're here? Like right in my neighborhood? My baby brother is right here? Could you be the answer to my prayers?"

That was heavy.

"Can we come by?"

"Shit, yes!" That's my girl. "I can't believe this. Johnnie, my brother! Do you need directions?"

OK . . . I had just told her we drove past her house, but I'd let that question slide. I thought it was probably just the excitement of hearing from me.

"Nope, really, we're just a couple blocks down the street."

"At Pete's?"

I stepped back from the building from which the pay phone was hanging and saw that the sign over the door said Pete's Liquors. The paint job looked like it had a bad case of dandruff.

"Yep, we're at Pete's."

"Hey, while you're there, grab a bottle of something strong so we can celebrate."

The tingling started at my Achilles heel and began working its way up the back of my leg. I didn't bother to ask what we were celebrating, as I assumed it was our reunion. Or maybe Christmas or New Year's or Kwanzaa.

"I think she's excited to see us," I said to Anna when I hopped back into the car. I had made a quick dash back into the liquor store and bought a bottle of what looked like a really nice little sparkling blanc de blanc. For the middle of the day, I thought it would be perfect. Maybe she would have some cheese and crackers out by the time we got there.

Anna just smiled at me and rested her hand on my arm again. I pulled away from the curb, turned the car around and headed back to my sister's house. In thirty seconds we were there, in front of the pale pink stucco bungalow. I parked at the curb and turned off the car.

"You sure you're up to this?" I asked Anna.

"Wouldn't miss meeting my sister-in-law for the world," she replied.

I sat for a moment, taking in the scene, trying to overlook the shabby front porch with a beat-up couch on one end and a broken planter with a dead palm on the other. The front door was open, and I wanted to take that as a welcome sign, but in my heart, I knew it was more probable that the last person through it had simply not thought to close it. Oh, hell, probably the last thirty people hadn't closed it, and nobody gave a damn. It's not like they need doors in Florida to keep out the cold. They're really just more of a formality. So maybe Janice wanted some fresh air, and maybe she had opened it as soon as she got my call.

I suddenly dropped my head in my hands and breathed as deeply as I could, because I thought I was going to pass out. There were warning signs everywhere, but we had come this far. How bad could it be— a reunion with my sister after so many years? If you can see what's coming, your crystal ball is much better than mine was that day.

"Come on, Mr. Family Man," Anna laughed. "She's your sister. How bad can it be?" Anna's crystal ball wasn't working so well, either.

By the time I got out of the car, Janice was standing in the doorway of her house. I could have passed this woman on the streets a dozen times and never have recognized her. If she had robbed me at knife-point, I could not have identified her in a lineup. My sister. Flesh and blood. Same parents. Remarkable.

Janice had always been thin, and I expected that years spent fighting substance abuse and poverty would have left her looking worn and rangy. But she was big. She had put on probably fifty pounds since I'd last seen her, and her hair hung long and stringy past her shoulders. I anticipated sunken cheeks and gray skin, but this woman was round and pink and smiling. She was wearing a pair of sweatpants that had been cut off above the knee and a tank top with "JEALOUS?" written across the chest. I suddenly thought this person must be a friend, someone there to greet us while Janice was freshening up, given that we had sprung this visit on her so suddenly. But when the arms opened, I knew it was she. Oh my.

"Johnnie!" she shouted, as we walked up to the porch. "Merry Christmas, baby!"

Baby?

"Did you bring the booze, hon?"

That's the way she opened the conversation. I looked from Janice to John and back to Janice, trying to see some kind of similarity in them— bone structure, eyes, hairline, nose, anything. But there was nothing. Janice was sweaty and smelled like the morning after at a frat house. Stale everything, and sweet pot smoke, but she was as friendly as they get. She wrapped her arms around John and then released him and came for me. I got the same warm hug. Then she stood back and started to apologize.

"But Johnnie, don't you wish that's the way Mom and Dad would have treated us when we were growing up? Well, that's the way we greet each other at the mission, and I guess I've just gotten used to it. Never can have too many hugs as far as I'm concerned! How are you, hon?"

My sister had adopted a Southern accent, which floored me. Yet the lazy way she talked seemed to fit right in with the rundown house and the clothes and who knows what other surprises we were in for. We headed inside.

"Johnnie, you got married, and you didn't even invite me?"

"We didn't invite anyone, Janice," I lied. Thirty seconds in her presence, and already my first lie. "We eloped." Lie number two.

"Nice going. You still in Michigan?"

"Yep. We live in a little town called Carlston."

"What did you bring from Pete's?"

I showed her the blanc de blanc, which stopped her cold.

"What is this?"

"It's a sparkling wine. You said you wanted to celebrate, and I thought this might be just the thing for the middle of the day."

The mood suddenly changed. Janice ran her hands over the bottle and looked a bit panicked. I, of course, thought she was put off by the screw top.

"It's OK," I said, taking the bottle from her and peeling off the foil. "A lot of the new sparkling wines have a screw top to prevent cork taint. Point me to some glasses."

"You got any money, John?" She stopped, and then started right up again. "Because here's the way it is. I got rent due on the 1st, and Louie here . . ."

Oh my God, we hadn't even seen the guy camped out on the couch. He was absolutely motionless, and my first thought was that Janice needed cash to bury him.

". . . Louie here hasn't been able to work because some jerk fingered him in a holdup, and the cops have been looking for him. He can't show his face until he grows out a beard. The folks at the mission have been telling me that God provides . . ." Lord, where had I heard that before?

". . . so when you called, I believed that you were sent straight here to help us out a bit. This blankety-blank"—I'm sure she meant blanc de blanc "—is . . . sweet . . . Johnnie, but what we really need is something hard, or Louie here is going to start shaking in a couple hours and getting real ugly. What do you say, baby brother? Can you go back to Pete's and grab something with a little color? Pete knows what we like. And while you're at it, he's got a little bag of stuff under the counter that he's been waiting for us to pick up, too."

Anna edged a bit closer to me and reached for my hand. I looked at her to see if she wanted to run, but she wasn't going anywhere. She had moved in to steady me. In my other hand, I still held the bottle of sparkling wine.

"Janice, what about rehab?" She had just given me what I assumed to be the better part of her mind, so I felt I could give her a piece of mine.

"Shit, John, a bunch of whining babies, just like Mom and Dad, you know? All talk. This is better. Louie and I . . . we got it made here. I get a disability check once a month, and the mission has been real good to

114

us. They say we're exactly the kind of people they want to help. So we let them. You know, they brought us a turkey just before Christmas, and I made us a real good dinner. We got friends here, and when Louie's working, we can keep ourselves real happy. We just hit a little speed bump these last couple months, and I was hoping you could help out."

Janice leaned over to the coffee table next to the sleeping Louie, picked up a partially smoked joint and held it out to me like an offering.

"This is unbelievably easy to get down here, John. People grow it in their bathrooms with artificial lights, and it's good stuff."

"I thought you went straight, Janice. Isn't that what you wanted?"

She took a deep breath.

"It's what everybody wants, John, until the next time somebody puts a hit in front of you. It wasn't worth the fight."

We heard the couch springs creak. Like a dead man rising on cue, Louie slowly sat up, and that was when I noticed the gun in his lap. He looked from Janice to me to Anna, blinked a few times and wrapped his right hand around what looked like a .38 pistol.

"Louie, this is my brother, John, and his wife, from Michigan."

There was a terrible silence while Louie clearly struggled through some fog to make sense of the strange man and woman in his living room.

"It's my brother, Louie. Go back to sleep, hon. We'll have some stuff for you when you wake up again."

Louie shook his head like a wet dog, then eased back down into the tattered couch. I thought he had passed out. His right arm slipped silently to the floor, and the gun slid out of his hand. Eyes still shut, he fumbled around the floor with his fingers until he located it, grabbed the barrel and laid it up on his chest. The recovery of his weapon took him less than eight seconds.

I looked at Janice, to see if she was afraid or shocked or embarrassed, but there was nothing. Her eyes were vacant. This little scene, I gathered, was commonplace, and it hadn't fazed her. For the moment, I found that comforting.

Janice, Anna and I have room in our house in Michigan if you would like to come live with us. We're leaving to go back in a few days, and I'll be happy to buy you a ticket so you can join us. We have a good life in Carlston, and I think you would like it there. You can make a new start.

115

That's what I wanted to say. This was my big sister, the girl who carried me home the day I fell off my bike and bloodied my knees, who ran interference when the older kids bullied me and when Mom was on the warpath. But I knew that Carlston was not what Janice needed or wanted, and neither were we. Contrary to her suggestion, we were not the answer to her prayers. In fact, our showing up on her doorstep wasn't even on her radar screen. She would have bear-hugged anybody she thought was bringing tequila and money to keep away the wild dogs. I could not save her. She'd have to get herself out of this. Or not.

We locked eyes for just a moment.

"Good-bye, Janice," I said. Anna's hand tightened in mine. In unison, we turned and walked out the door through which we had come less than ten minutes earlier. Janice was silent. Louie snored. We walked across the porch, down the steps and across the grass. Anna whispered "I'm in," meaning, "Don't take the time to come around to my side of the car and open the door for me. Just get in, and let's get the hell out of here."

Seven

  OK . . . so you want to know what happened when we drove away? There really weren't the histrionics that you might assume, given that we had just faced a drunk guy with a gun, on the run from the cops, and his girlfriend who was looking for a fix. John and I were silent while he drove about ten blocks. Then he pulled into a grocery store parking lot, found an empty space far away from other cars and stopped. He slid his hands together at the top of the steering wheel and pressed his forehead against them. The bottle of blanc de blanc lay between us on the seat—the only tangible evidence of the reunion gone awry.

"Anna, I'm so sorry . . ."

I leaned over and wrapped my arms around him. He was shaking.

"I'm so sorry I put you in danger, Anna. I never dreamed that's what we would walk into."

"You know, John, I don't really think we were in any immediate danger," I said, thinking back to the besotted boyfriend. I had been so focused on listening for the sound of John's heart breaking as we stood in Janice's living room that I really hadn't thought much about the idiot on the couch. "My guess is that the gun wasn't loaded, and even if it was, what are the chances that Louie would have shot at us, given that he's trying to lay low until he grows a beard?"

Suddenly that sounded terribly funny to me, and I started to laugh. "John, was that really your sister? My sister-in-law? You know, maybe

117

if she would have just tasted the wine, she would have appreciated the effort you put into selecting it, with, you know, the fruity bouquet and overtones of shag carpet and gun smoke. Oh, my God."

"I'm sorry," John said again. His face was red and wet when he looked up at me.

"I know, honey. Not in our wildest dreams could we have anticipated that little scene. Let it go, John. We're fine, as good as we were before this afternoon, and maybe better. You had so many questions about Janice before today, and now you have answers. And I know they're painful, but if anything, maybe this afternoon will reassure you that your decision to cut her out of your life years ago was the right thing to do."

"And what now?"

"Well . . . now we go back and tell Mike the whole sordid story—and don't leave out a single detail. He will love it, of course, and telling him will make us feel better, because while this feels pretty awful right now, someday, maybe even by this evening, we will find ourselves laughing about it. I think. And each time we tell the story, Louie's gun will get bigger. By the time we get back to Carlston, he will have brandished a semiautomatic deer rifle."

"And Janice?"

"Hmmm, well . . . I think we'll remember her for her big hugs and the great sadness in her life. She tried, John. She's just one of so many who don't make it out the other side of rehab. Then there is you, my hero. Steady Eddy. But I have to tell you . . . I was starting to lay odds you were going to invite her to come live with us."

"Yeah, well I thought about it. We have her address. Maybe I can write to her. Maybe things will change for her someday. Maybe I can help her with rent."

"Of course, John. And there's plenty of time to think about that. Right now, I vote we head home to Mike's and put this behind us."

I brushed John's damp hair from his forehead. I knew he was crushed. He rubbed his face across the sleeve of his polo shirt, and sat back in his seat. Then he reached across and took my hand. He smiled a little and called me his rock. I know this about us. John is strong and creative and emotional. Day to day, he holds us together. But flick him with your finger when he is hurt, and he can crumble like a sand castle at high tide. This afternoon I was the strong one.

About thirty quiet minutes later, we pulled into Mike's driveway and felt great relief to see him step out the front door and walk toward the car, waving happily to us. Could he have known? It was barely five p.m.

Mike had decided to make a traditional Cuban supper that evening, and when he greeted us at the car, I could smell the wonderful spiciness of it on his shirt.

"You're back pretty quickly," he said, putting a fatherly arm around John. "You OK?" Then he looped his other arm through mine and the three of us walked across the lawn toward the house.

"Yeah," was all John said.

"I made a pitcher of sangria," Mike said, letting go of us as we walked inside. The aromas from a simmering pot of black bean stew and a platter of fried sweet plantain surrounded us. "How about a glass?"

John nodded silently, then pulled out a chair at the kitchen table and sat down.

"That sounds fabulous, Mike," I replied, a bit forced. I watched John form his arms into a cradle on the table and rest his head on them.

"Not such a good meeting, pal?" Mike asked gently, holding out the sangria when John looked up at him.

"Oh my God, Mike. Worse than I ever imagined. It was a horrible mistake to go there. Janice is a mess, and she's got this mess of a boyfriend who had a gun." John looked at me and slowly started to grin. "A semiautomatic deer rifle . . ."

"And you didn't invite them for supper?" Mike asked, raising his eyebrows like the very thought of coming home without them was incredible. Then he patted John's shoulder. "Well, old boy, I'd say you exercised extreme good sense!"

"I nearly wet my pants."

"Yeah, I imagine you did. Unexpected encounters with weaponry can do that to a guy." Then he turned to me.

"You OK, Anna?"

John answered first. "She didn't even flinch."

"I'm fine. Better now," I said, taking the glass Mike offered. "And John, just for the record, I'd like to know if you have any other long-lost relatives you want to introduce me to, because I'm thinking that maybe I'll pass on an invitation to the next family reunion . . ."

119

Mike started laughing at that, and so did John, who uttered something about marrying for better or worse. After bowls of beans and rice and plates of fried sweet plantain with ice cream, the three of us took a walk to a little park just a few blocks from Mike's house. Mike brought along an old blanket and spread it on a grassy area away from the streetlights.

"I come here often to look at the stars," he said, lying down on his back and inviting us to do the same. We pointed out the stars we could identify and the constellations we remembered learning in elementary school. Big Dipper. Orion the Hunter. Ursa Major. When we ran out of those we knew, we made up new ones. Garden Shovel. Car with No Tires. French Toast.

"Sandy pulled a knife on me near the end of our marriage," Mike said, without the slightest shift in tone. "I had surprised her by following her to a party—surprising her was never a safe thing to do. I tracked her to a house, walked right in and found her in the kitchen with a bunch of people I didn't know. I told her I had come to take her home. She swore at me, and picked up a big French knife that was lying on the counter in front of her. She pointed it at me and told me to leave her alone. I remember being shocked—not really scared, but shocked. I realized we had come to the end, so I left, and the next day I filed papers to keep her away from the girls. It turned out not to be necessary. She never came back home, never asked for them, never even asked to see them.

"When I look up into the sky, I feel connected to everybody else on this earth . . . people in Alaska, in India, in the tiniest villages in Russia and Africa and people at the Poles. I feel the significance of every flower and every bug and bird . . . of every coyote and deer and . . . elephant. I feel connected to all of it. And even though I don't know exactly how we all got here or what happens when we die, when I look up at the stars, I feel that everything is here for a purpose—a very precious purpose. And I am part of it all. I find that comforting."

So did I.

John and I were making quiet love that night when John suddenly began to cry again. It didn't surprise me. John started to apologize, then rolled over and faced the wall.

"Hey, you. Roll back over here," I told him. "I'm not finished with you yet."

"Anna, I can't . . ."

"John, that's not what I mean. Roll over, and look at me."

His face was flushed, and he just looked so sad. To see this devastation in him twice in one day nearly did me in. I knew there was nothing I could say to make him feel better. Today would stay with him for a long time. But at least it was a memory we would share. This one would not be his to bear alone. I put my arm over him and kissed his eyes. Crying can be a very good thing. Women know this. Sometimes a good cry can begin to heal a heart full of hurt.

Eight

🍃 *With New Year's Eve upon us, Mike asked what we'd like to do to celebrate.* As you know by now, John and I are not big party people, and we were tired. Mike is not big on raucous parties either, and I think for most New Year's Eves, he had spent a quiet evening at home, usually alone, reflecting on his life and his great good fortune to have three fine daughters and a beautiful bungalow in Florida. So when we each voiced preferences for a New Year's celebration, our thoughts were remarkably similar. Good food at home, great champagne at home and a walk to the beach around midnight. And that is exactly what we did.

It was a perfect tropical night. The moon was a waning crescent in a cloudless sky, so the stars were especially bright. The waves were calm, and the breezes that had made their way around the world passed lightly across my face and arms as soft as down. I can never feel wind without wondering from where it has traveled, and who or what last inhaled the same elusive molecules I am drawing into my lungs.

We strolled along the sand, the three of us arm in arm with Mike in the middle, and then he suggested a game of telling the punch lines of jokes—just the punch lines.

"For example," he offered, "he got an erection and fell off his perch."

Well, as you can imagine, John loved this idea immediately and jumped right in.

122

"But Eno, what will I tell my Sunday-school class?"

And with that, we were off. After a few minutes of resurrecting numerous disconnected endings, we were laughing so hard we got sidesplits and couldn't go on. This game gets funny very quickly. In fact, it's not really a game. Everybody just starts yelling out the ends of jokes like, "My dear, I think your hearing aids need new batteries" or "I'm the designated decoy." And my favorite, "Super callused fragile mystic hexed by halitosis." Get it?

OK . . . maybe you had to be there. It was hilarious. Anyway our silliness exhausted us, so we sat down on the cool sand and looked out at the ocean. I felt a sense of contentment that had all but disappeared since our early, innocent days at Maple Hill. I was optimistic and a bit tipsy, heading toward magnanimous.

"Thank you for writing to us, Mike," I said, feeling the weight of months of unanswered questions leaping lightly off my shoulders one by one, rolling toward the water and disappearing into the surf.

"And thank you for inviting us here," John chimed in.

Mike put an arm around each of us.

"You have been a gift to me, you know," he said, with his characteristic grace. "I've been wondering about Mary's beginnings for a very long time. If it turns out that our Mary is your Rose, and everything is certainly pointing in that direction, we will all have found a lot of answers this week. You were very brave to accept my offer to come visit. I am grateful to you, and I cannot remember a better holiday in years."

He paused for a moment and looked up at the stars, from which, I was beginning to understand, he drew strength and clarity. "I told you earlier that I don't know what happens to us when we die, but I do believe in some kind of afterlife. And I think that the people who need to find each other, do. If what we suspect is true, perhaps Jeanette and Mary-Rose have been instrumental in getting us together."

Well, he was right on one account. Jeanette was certainly responsible for our search, though I wasn't about to give her credit for our meeting Mike. His daughter could take bows for that. I couldn't even guess Mary's role in this, nor her influence on our search. In truth, I never even thought about it. Trying to understand the motives and powers of *one* dead woman was plenty for me.

John and I breathed in the warm air and let Mike's words settle quietly around us for a minute or two. Then John said with reverence, "And the tail of the camel is used to make Camel cigarettes."

~ *Anna and I had spent the week with Mike as any three comfortable old* friends might. That we were practically strangers was remarkable, and added to my feeling that we had come to the right place at the right time. Mike worked around the house doing a chore or two every day—painting wrought iron, pruning the orchard, repairing disintegrating stucco. I joined him usually, and though I'd had little interest in or time for making the repairs our own house needed, working side by side with Mike was pure pleasure. The three of us ate supper together, and often cooked together. We also took a daily walk together. We fell into an easy routine from the first day, though none of us planned it that way. At Mike's suggestion, we went to a local marine sanctuary where we could swim with dolphins and visited a nursery that specializes in cacti. I checked email and put in a couple hours of wine work most mornings. Anna indulged in a pedicure and a manicure, then got a massage and a facial, and announced one afternoon that she thought she might look into opening a spa in Carlston. We joked that she would be its most frequent client.

On our first full day at Mike's house, we spread out on a large table in the living room all the photos the three of us had gathered of Rose and Mary, Martin and Jeanette, and all of Mike's immediate family, along with all the notes and articles we had about Jeanette and the disappearance of Rose. Each of us spent a bit of time there during the week, usually by ourselves, looking everything over, searching for puzzle pieces that fit. On the night before our departure, we found ourselves there together for a few hours, sorting and talking and hypothesizing. There were no photos of Mary as an infant—nothing that we could compare to the one photo we had of Rose. While we thought we saw similarities between Rose's baby picture and a shot of Mary as a five-year-old going off to kindergarten, we knew that we really *wanted* to see similarities. And we also knew that a tiny swaddled baby wearing a bonnet would look considerably different just a few months later, given that babies grow so quickly. Even hair and eye color can change after birth.

We also compared the photos of Mary as an adult to the images of Martin and Jeanette, looking for clues of their relationship in the arch of an eyebrow, the fullness of lips and the angle of a cheekbone. Nothing jumped out at us, but then, the photos of Martin and Jeanette were old and faded, and both looked terribly stern, as was typical of early poses. I guess nobody ever thought to tell them to say "cheese."

Almost as an afterthought, on that last evening, Mike asked how we had come to know about Rose and what prompted our search for her.

Anna and I had discussed whether or not we'd tell Mike the story, and had not come to any conclusion. We'd wait and see, we decided. Wait until we were brave enough to share this bizarre tale . . . and see if we thought he was the kind of person who would accept it or send us packing. Now that he had posed the question, I had no qualms about answering. You know when you develop a friendship with someone, and you feel that deep, shared sense of trust and camaraderie? That's what Anna and I both felt with Mike. It was irrelevant that we had known him only a month.

Fueled with respect and fondness for our new friend, and with a desire to unload the grim journey that brought us to his home, I started talking.

"Jeanette is still very much . . . hmmm . . . *active* in our house, and she sort of accidentally . . . hmmm . . . got . . . inside Anna when she was trying to get our attention. And Anna nearly died, so we brought in Roberta, a . . . medium . . . who could talk to Jeanette and find out why she was sticking around and what she wanted from us. Roberta is pretty incredible. She said Jeanette told her the story of Rose's abduction, and Jeanette said . . . well, I don't know if *said* is the right word, but anyway, she *conveyed* to Roberta that she was trying to get our attention so that we would find out for her what had happened to her baby. Jeanette's story was corroborated with the articles we found in the paper, so we started on this search to get Jeanette some answers so she can leave our house and move on.

"Anna nearly died, Mike. We didn't have any choice but to pursue every lead we could find."

It was pretty quiet after I spit out this thirty-second summation of the last eighteen months of our lives. I hadn't rehearsed what I'd say. It just, literally, spilled out. I guess I felt it was best not to try to be coy. The real surprise was not my spontaneous little speech, but rather Mike's reaction to it. He took this big deep breath, smiled as though to himself and shook his head a bit.

"Mary once told me that when she was quite young, but old enough to be aware of what was going on around here, she thought she heard her mother—her birth mother—crying for her."

Later that evening, while John was packing, I went out to the lanai and stared up at the stars, trying to imagine what it was like for Jeanette in her last days. A young mother, widowed, alone and ill, she had struggled to keep her little family together in the face of what appeared to us to have been a small conspiracy against the unsaved. She lost her daughter to thieves, and her son to her in-laws. Perhaps it wasn't the flu at all that had killed her. Perhaps, like Pearl, she had died of an attack of heart.

The one thing we had hoped to do, when we started our search for Rose, was to also find Jeanette's grave. That had not happened. And that did not surprise us. We never located an obituary that might have given date and location of burial, and her name did not appear in the records of any local cemeteries. We wondered if Jeanette had been befriended by the local Ottawa or Ojibwa people; if that was the case, they may have accepted her body for burial in their own graveyard. That would have been unusual, but not out of the question. It would, however, mean we would likely never find her. The area's earliest inhabitants did not mark graves in traditional ways we recognized.

We knew there were also two small paupers' fields just outside of town, where dozens of the poor, and those whom no one claimed, were buried quickly and with little ceremony. Records on them, too, were often informal, and their wooden crosses and grave markers deteriorated quickly in the elements.

It is hard for those of us who have not been through an epidemic similar to the Spanish influenza of 1918 and 1919 to imagine the fear that gripped towns when otherwise healthy young people began bleeding from the eyes and nose and were dead in days, sometimes hours. Unlike other illnesses that took the youngest and the oldest, this flu took an unprecedented number of strong, young adults. Researchers now know that they often fell victim for the very reason they survived other illnesses—their strong immune systems put up too great a fight and left them vulnerable to opportunistic infection and—most terrifying—a breakdown in skin tissue. Many flu victims bled to death.

Still, it was hard not to judge. Had Jeanette's in-laws abandoned her after she died? Did they not even give her a proper funeral and gravestone? She was the mother of their grandchildren, for God's sake.

I also wondered if it was possible that Martin's parents had provided for her burial but declined to make the arrangements public. Their social standing appears to have been in jeopardy by their very association with Jeanette, and showing their sympathy—or even the barest elements of respect—might have raised more eyebrows than they cared to confront. Optimistically, I hoped that they had sent her body to Canada to be buried next to Martin.

I wished desperately to know if Jeanette had been the topic of conversation over tea, and if her in-laws eventually told Andre the truth about his family.

John had tried to unearth more about Rose's big brother, but he came across little. He was hoping for information about his life after military service, but privacy issues prohibited our looking through military files. We knew it was even possible that Andre was still alive. He didn't have longevity in his genes, but maybe he had beaten the odds. That evening, I added some more unanswered questions to the list of things I no longer cared about, any more than I cared about the color of Pearl's dress the day she decided that she was an instrument of God.

Mike now belonged to our small fraternity of people who knew the whole story. We filled him in on every unbelievable detail, starting with the photos of Jeanette and her family that I hung on our walls, and right through the serendipitous meeting with Roberta and her silent chats with Jeanette. It was hard to believe, but it seemed, at last, this whole scary drama was about to be over. Mike had no doubt that it was baby Rose whom Pearl had placed tenderly in Ella's arms—the wonderful sister he adored, who was all grown up by the time he was born. He felt there were too many similarities to be simply coincidences.

And what of the question as to who actually took Rose from the porch and how Pearl acquired her? Well, I hope this doesn't disappoint you, but we let that alone. Mostly. We did not know and figured we never would. It was that simple. And the options for who and how seemed to number as many as the stars that we had come to love in those clear Tampa night skies. As far as we were concerned, it was a curious detail, but not essential information to satisfy Jeanette. Mike confirmed that Pearl had, indeed, been surrounded by people who might have taken the child to save her soul—or even just to save her life, if they felt she was not being properly tended to. He included the righteous Walter in that group. But even for Mike, it was a detail that could remain unsolved. I think we were all reluctant to incriminate people who had been dead for decades. And it was not lost on us that while Rose's abduction had a devastating impact on Jeanette, it probably saved Ella's life.

Eight days after arriving in Tampa, we boarded a plane and headed home. When we left Mike's house that morning, he had pressed into John's hands a large manila envelope that contained duplicate photos of Mary, along with photos of himself with his daughters. We were very touched, and promised to make him copies of our photos of Rose and Martin and Jeanette as well, and send them back to him.

I was ready for a party, a big one. But there was a problem. There were few people with whom we had shared our secret, so it would be a gathering of four—John, me, Roberta and Grace. I wanted to sing and dance until dawn. We were about to reclaim our house and set free the spirit of one very old and very desperate mother. The only discouraging part of our homecoming was that I suddenly seemed to have caught a nasty cold, which I assumed I had picked up in the few hours we spent at a mall near Mike's house, shopping for gifts to bring back to friends.

～ *Did you wonder, when Anna mentioned that she was sick again, if I panicked? Of course I did. Thank you, Pavlov.*

❧ *I trusted John. I need to start by saying that. We'd been married only a short time, but we had known each other for years, and the big things that attracted me to him early on were his honesty, his sense of fairness and his steady response to the stuff that life throws at us. His reaction to Janice didn't surprise me. The fact that he had hoped—expected, really—to find her well and stable, and yet could turn and walk out the door when faced with a very different picture of his sister, was exactly what I expected from him. And that John's primary concern afterward was that he had put* me *at risk was also lovingly typical of him. Still . . . I was curious.*

I fell asleep in my seat while our plane going from Tampa to Detroit was still sitting on the warm tarmac, waiting for clearance to take off. About thirty minutes later, when we were well above the clouds, I awoke to find John staring out the window, the sun streaming in, an unopened book on his lap.

"You OK?" I asked him.

"Hey, my sleeping beauty," he responded, smiling at me. "Have a good nap?"

"Did I snore?"

"Yeah. Not so loud though. More like little snorts . . . and wheezes. And you kicked your legs a couple times. The guy in the seat in front of you asked the flight attendant if he could move to another part of the plane."

I leaned forward and tried to see if anyone was in the seat. It was empty. But the plane was only about half full, so the guy I saw sit down there when we first boarded could very well have decided to move to a row where he'd have more room. "You are kidding me, aren't you?"

"Noooo . . . not me. Not about anything this important." John laughed and reached an arm around me. He pressed his face against mine and whispered in my ear, "You know I would never kid you about something so serious . . ."

"OK, then . . . speaking of serious, I have a question for you." It had been on my mind since the morning before, when I woke up early with visions of .38 specials dancing in my head.

"John, what would it have taken for you to decide you wanted to offer to help Janice? Like, the rent money, for example. She said her rent was due. It can't be more than a few hundred dollars. We could afford that. Did you consider giving it to her?" There was a bit of a pause, and John slowly shook his head.

"No. And not because it was anything I thought about beforehand. I expected to find Janice in good shape, so when she asked me for money, I was pretty surprised. Remember, I was the one who thought she might bring out cheese and crackers. But after the first couple minutes there, I realized that probably none of the things I anticipated were going to happen."

"Things like . . . ?"

"I don't know . . . maybe just finding the sister who last wrote to me and told me she was back on her feet."

John turned toward the window again. It was sunny above the

clouds. All sunny and bright. I always marveled, when I flew, at that dream world above the clouds. It could be raining cats and dogs on the earth below, but up there, all was peaceful. John turned back to me.

"I think that any money I gave Janice would have gone from her hand to Pete's cash drawer, don't you?"

"OK, so hypothetically"—I know John hates hypothetical discussions, but I was digging in—"how about if Louie hadn't been in the picture?"

"Do you mean what if it was Janice there asking for money? No Louie, no gun? No joint? No request for tequila? No mention of the stuff Pete's keeping under the counter for her?"

"Do you think that's all Louie's influence?"

"I don't know. I guess I'd like to believe that. That's why I thought about asking Janice to come back to Michigan with us. It crossed my mind briefly . . . very briefly, that maybe she didn't really want that lifestyle but didn't know how to get away from it. And with Louie lying there with a gun, I wondered if maybe he had threatened her or something if she talked about leaving him. I know that happens, and I thought maybe that's what was going on. Hell . . . maybe that *is* what's going on. Do you think I should have made the offer?"

Janice had made it very clear that she liked her life just fine. And if she felt beholden to keep Louie supplied, well, she certainly came by that instinct naturally. She had cared for John when they were young, and she had tried to care for her parents when their marriage was rocky and the daily grind wore them down. When she was still a kid in junior high school, John said she talked about wanting to be a social worker. John had the same instincts, but he knew enough to save himself first.

"I think you made the right decision—for you. But I'm just wondering at what point you might have decided to try to help her. I mean, all the time you read about relatives who go out on a limb to help each other, and then they find out that the destitute brother they moved into their house has been doing drugs and raped their daughter, or steals something valuable and disappears, or kills his parents. Or, you know, the guy who takes his brother's side in a lawsuit and finds out the loser really did hold up the liquor store. There was a story in the paper when we were at Mike's about a couple who told their daughter she couldn't live with them anymore because she lied all the time and cut school and had sex. They wanted to do the tough-love thing, and a couple months later, the police found the girl about fifteen pounds thinner, huddled in a box in an alley."

John started to chuckle. "Anna, you need some new reading material . . ."

This got under my skin. The whole idea of blood being thicker than water, and family standing up for family, lying for them, protecting them and taking all kinds of risks for them . . . it troubled me. I used to think that I would have done anything for my grandparents, and given them anything asked for, but now, I'm not sure. And thankfully, I was never tested. We had an incredibly easy life together. I'd like to say it was pretty "normal," but who knows what that means anymore? They never once asked me to rob a bank or sleep with an important client or be devious in any way. And they never needed my help getting out of a jam. They were just good, middle-class, Midwestern folks trying to make a happy life for their orphaned granddaughter.

"I still wonder about Jeanette and what she might have done out of love for her children. I know this is old territory, but the question keeps creeping back into my mind. How far would Jeanette have gone to protect them? I don't think Rose was stolen in the way that Jeanette would have us believe. I keep going back to the idea that Jeanette might have given her away because she saw her own death coming, and then made up the story about the abduction in the hope of gaining some sympathy from the town. We know she was already ill. . . . maybe she just wasn't thinking straight. Maybe she was so sick that she didn't remember sending Rose away, and that's why she thinks the baby was stolen."

"That occurred to me, too," John said, "but I would have thought that when Jeanette died, she would have become aware, and she would know what had happened to Rose. I don't think there would have been any reason for her to stick around. And if she would have given the baby to a family nearby, they certainly would have spoken up at some point, wouldn't they?"

"You're probably right. Maybe the biggest sacrifice she made for Rose was staying around for the last ninety years to find her. It's so sad that none of the earlier owners got the message from her like we did. Imagine how wonderful it would have been to find Rose still alive and to bring her back to the house. I wonder what a ghost does to celebrate."

"Yeah, maybe they serve Grey Ghost vodka martinis . . ."

"It's called Grey Goose, not ghost, John. Stick with wine. It's what you know."

"Oh," John said with a smile that meant that with a little encouragement he would start on a list of ghost-related foods that one would serve at such a party.

I beat him to it. "They might serve chips and salsa."

"Salsa?" he asked.

"Medium hot."

"And for entertainment, they would play recordings of Unchained Melody."

John and I could milk a subject like this for minutes at a time on a long car ride. But for the moment I still had Jeanette and Janice on my mind.

"John, how far would you go for your child . . . no, forget that. How far would you go for your sister?"

"You mean, like, would I try to find Janice a good family to live with and then hang around as a ghost for a century trying to find out what happened to her?"

I sighed and closed my eyes.

"OK, you want a serious answer? Because I've been thinking about this, too. The whole thing with Janice makes me feel bad in so many ways, but this is the conclusion I've come to. If I thought at any point I could make a difference . . . some kind of real and lasting difference in Janice's life, I'd probably try to do something. But here's the catch. I'm not willing to put you at risk for anybody—not even my sister. So the thought of bringing her into our home and worrying about whether Louie was still somewhere in the background—I wouldn't even consider it. If I thought Janice was helpless . . . that might be different. I might feel the need to protect her. But this is a girl who has been carving up her life for a long time. She's making decisions, Anna. She's an adult, and I'm not going to interfere."

"So what if she asked you for something other than money? What if she had slipped you a piece of paper so that Louie wouldn't know? What if she gave you a note that said, 'Help me get out of here'? What would you have done?"

"Anna . . . this is getting tedious. I don't know what I would have done. This is all so hypothetical."

"Humor me, John. What if Janice called next week and asked if she

132

could come live with us for a while until she got on her feet? And what if she made it clear she was leaving Louie behind?"

John looked out the window again. We were starting our descent into Detroit, and the view was obscured by huge gray clouds.

"Just like that?" John asked. "Like, 'Hello, John, this is Janice. I'm leaving Louie, the bum on the couch with the gun. Can I come live with you and Anna?'"

Suddenly the plane dropped like an overloaded elevator. I let out a yell with the rest of the passengers. The plane felt like it was flying across the tops of boulders.

"There are storms all around Detroit," John said, taking my hand.

The pilot came over the speakers and told us to make sure our seatbelts were securely fastened. He apologized for the sudden turbulence being caused by high winds and snow squalls, and he said the next few minutes were going to be a bit bumpy.

"Shit," John said quietly. "I hate flying."

⁓ *When we arrived in Grand Rapids, Anna was tempted to call Roberta* from the airport. We wanted her to know as soon as possible that it was time for her to come back and give Jeanette the good news. But it was late. Too late, we decided. Instead, Anna waited for our luggage while I went to get our car. The weather in Michigan had deteriorated while we were gone, to the point that even polar bears might have been disheartened, and the ride home from the Grand Rapids airport was slow and slick. It felt ridiculously cold, and I entertained momentary thoughts of selling our house and buying the cute Spanish-style bungalow I'd seen for sale around the corner from Mike.

We were tired to the bone, and we were emotional wrecks, veering between the stress of our search and the realization that we had answers. Anna and I hauled our suitcases into the house, and Anna headed for bed without giving a single thought to looking at the mail, unpacking toothbrushes or even pouring a glass of wine. She was already tucked under her comforter and heading toward REMs when I finished checking the house, went upstairs and pulled off my clothes, which still smelled like sunscreen. I thought about how it had been seventy-four degrees earlier that day in Florida. I curled up close to Anna and closed my eyes, comforted by the sound of the furnace motor. I wanted to sleep for a week.

⁊ *Home felt good. John and I slept late, and when I finally crawled out of* bed around nine a.m., it was only to make a pot of coffee for us and crawl back under the covers. The Weather Channel verified what we already knew—it was darn cold outside. So we surfed around the cable channels and found a great old Jimmy Stewart movie in progress, plumped up our pillows and snuggled in to watch it. We really didn't have a good reason to get up. I had to agree with John that much as we both like winter, a week of seventy-five-degree days had spoiled us. It would take a while for me to remember what I found appealing about gray, cold and snow.

Around 10:30, while the movie credits were rolling, I phoned Roberta at the café to tell her the good news, and was dismayed to learn that she was out of town. She was attending a two-week work-shop in New Mexico on healing arts and wouldn't be back for several days. The staff at the café had been asked not to disturb her unless there was an emergency. I wondered if getting Jeanette out of the house qualified as an emergency. John was philosophical.

"We'll talk to her when she gets back, Anna," he said, "and mean-while, we can get all these articles and photos filed and get caught up on laundry, and talk about where you want to go on vacation."

"Vacation? Isn't that what we just got back from?"

"Sort of. But it was a working vacation. I'm ready for one that's all play. And no family reunions . . ."

We had made the assumption that Roberta would come back to the house for a few days to talk to Jeanette so she could tell her what we learned about Rose. And John thought we ought to leave while that was happening. I wasn't real keen on staying around myself, but had thought more in terms of taking a long weekend in Chicago.

"How about Arizona?" John asked. "Neither of us has been there before, and we know it's pretty and warm. I was thinking we could fly out and find a cabin or apartment near Sedona and explore the area for a week or so. What do you think?"

Truthfully, since I had been home less than twelve hours, the thought of heading out again didn't thrill me. But I figured it would be a few weeks before Roberta could come for a visit, and by then I'd be ready. Besides, the thought of sitting around wondering if Jeanette was going to push for attention again was totally unappealing.

We passed our first few days at home doing exactly as John had suggested. We filed all the papers we had taken with us to Florida, plus the copies of documents and photos Mike had given us. We did laundry and repacked our warm-weather clothes in anticipation of a week in red rock country. John caught up with the wineries that had left nonurgent messages while we were gone. He also stopped by his travel agent and picked up some brochures that advertised everything from Jeep tours through the canyons to readings with spiritual advisors. Sedona, we discovered, is considered a very spiritual area. Now, I don't know exactly what that means, but it is populated with dozens of mediums and readers and spiritual advisors, and has a handful of shops that sell things like crystals and books and CDs and supplies for those who practice various forms of spiritualism. It also has a number of vortexes, which are geographic areas that register a particularly high energy level among those capable of feeling it.

I almost balked at the whole trip when I read about that last part. Get this: we were leaving our house because a medium was going to come and tell our resident ghost it was time for her to move on. And we were going to a place that draws people seeking mystical experiences and communion with the spiritual world. It seemed a bit redundant. Or something. Still, it did look like gorgeous country, and being a fan of Southwestern art, I was looking forward to wandering among Sedona's galleries.

There was one more task to be worked on. John made a trip to the post office our first afternoon home and returned with half a grocery bag of mail. Just because we believed we had found our baby Rose didn't mean the letters of inquiry stopped. We decided we'd get back into our routine of reading them to each other in the evening, and answering every one that seemed serious. By now, we had composed a form letter of sorts on the computer that made the process easier and took less of an emotional toll on us. We also pledged that in another week or so, we would cancel the post office box, so the letters would be returned to their senders. I didn't want to think what that might mean to someone desperate to find news of a loved one, but we wanted to put this slice of our life behind us.

Mike called on January 5. He missed us. And he had found a treasure. After we left, he did a little more sorting through boxes of old family stuff to see if he might have overlooked anything, and he came across a big family Bible that he believed had been given to his parents

135

by—who else—Walter and Pearl. When he opened it, he found a log of dates for births and deaths that had likely been kept by Ella. It contained the name of her firstborn twins who died in her arms. Birth and death on the same day. And birth dates for her three miracle children. Mary's birthday was recorded as February 14, 1919. Mike knew his parents had never learned the actual day of Mary's birth, and so they selected a date that symbolized their love for their new foundling: Valentine's Day.

He also found three tiny bundles of hair, each tied with a piece of ribbon, on which was written the name of the child to whom it had belonged. Mike, Megan, Mary. He wondered if maybe Mary's—a tiny, tangible remembrance loaded with DNA—would give Jeanette the proof she wanted.

❧ *Since Anna and I had nothing of Rose's, we could not do a cross-check* with the hair sample to verify that it belonged to the missing baby. Anna reminded me that these days, researchers can extract DNA from the most minute samples, but nine decades later, with no body, no clothes, no bloodstains or drool and no siblings or direct heirs, Mary's little curl was pretty useless from a researcher's vantage point. But Jeanette might feel differently about it, and in that lay our hope. Mike said he would send it by overnight mail to be sure we got it, if we thought it would be helpful to Roberta when she talked with Jeanette. I chuckled to myself at the suggestion. Do you see how we all had come to envision our resident spirit mother? I'm sure if you asked the three of us, we would each tell you that we thought of Jeanette as a complete presence in our house—a body, face, hair, clothes, boots, everything. The fact that we couldn't see her didn't mean she wasn't there. So given this vision, I could imagine Roberta reaching out a hand to the invisible Jeanette, offering her the dark beribboned ringlet. And I could see Jeanette taking it. I guess I'd come pretty far for a guy who wasn't allowed to believe in Santa. But then, I told myself with perfect logic, what mother wouldn't eagerly grasp the only material evidence she had of a lost child?

I got pretty excited thinking about this whole scene. Then I noticed Anna's less than enthusiastic reaction, and I realized that we had switched places at the research table over the past couple weeks. Anna, who had been so eager to get her hands on anything about our house and its history, and who was pretty determined when we began searching for clues about Rose, was now growing tired of the chase. I could understand that. We believed that Anna's health might depend on us winning the "Find Baby Rose" game, and the implications of that threat were almost unbearable to consider. However, I had been bit by the history bug, as Mike called it—and the symptoms included a huge hunger for details. More and more and more of them.

John is right. I didn't particularly want to talk about our search for Rose. I was done with it, except for the remaining task of giving Jeanette the information she wanted and sending her on her way. My motive was pretty self-serving. I wanted Jeanette gone. But John's interest in our mission grew. He had been shocked and also moved by the whole scary debacle with Janice. It gave him some insight into this universal desire that we humans have to connect with those who are, even in fragile, desperate ways, a part of us. Mike had been just a guy looking for information that might end the drama at our house, but he became a friend in search of a sister. When John realized he couldn't build a meaningful bridge with Janice, he channeled that energy into helping Mike sort out the details of his own sister's early life.

John's thoughts of Jeanette changed, too. When he spoke of her now, his tone was softer, tender. He understood, perhaps for the first time, the depth of Jeanette's love for her daughter and why it had held her earthbound for decades. He wanted so much to help her. So he took the lead and barely realized that I was so over this project.

You know what else? I was afraid. While John was bubbling all over about how cool it was that Mike had found a piece of Mary's hair, I started getting a sick feeling in my stomach. For starters, what if Jeanette looked at it, or touched it, or sensed it or whatever spirits do, and decided it didn't belong to Rose? Swell.

I confess I was also a bit creeped out by the hair. My grandparents once told me how Victorian women saved the hair from their brushes and combs and found wonderful uses for it. In fact, china and Bakelite dresser sets often included a receptacle, called a hair receiver, that had a hole in the top about the size of a quarter through which they would push the hair. And then, when they were done with barn chores and having tea, the women would do all sorts of creative things with that hair like braid it into necklaces or rings, or make flower pictures out of it. I swear I am not making this up. You can still find the pictures occasionally in antique stores. I think there must have been some hair swapping going on, too, because the flowers are usually made of different colors of hair. I used to be fascinated by it. I thought those women were so resourceful. Clearly the art form was a casualty of the bob, though you can find hair-receiver sets that were made and used well into the 1940s.

Roberta seemed a bit guarded when she got the news that we believed we'd found a warm trail to Rose and were about to receive a curl of hair that was likely hers. Mike guessed it had been clipped from her head when she was about five or six years old. Historians know how to date this stuff, I guess.

I was afraid at first that Roberta wasn't planning to come back and talk to Jeanette, but she brought it up.

"Is it time for me to come and have a chat with our friend?" she asked, when she called after returning from New Mexico. It was a much less celebratory—or perhaps enthusiastic—response than I had hoped to hear. I had marked on the calendar the date that Roberta was due back from her trip, and I decided I would give her up to two days past that to call us first. I didn't want to push, but neither did I feel like sitting around in my house waiting to get possessed again. In response to her question, I told Roberta that yes, it was time, that we had accumulated a substantial amount of information about Rose and had met her stepbrother, born later into her adopted family.

"Roberta, can you come up for the weekend?" I asked eagerly. "We'll tell you the whole story and show you all the photos. Rose had a good life and was surrounded by a great family. I think that Jeanette will be able to rest easy now, knowing that Rose was loved. I can't wait to share it all with you!"

Nine

$\sim$ *Anna and Roberta talked for several minutes about a proposed game* plan, and Anna brought up the idea of our leaving town for a few days while Roberta was here. Roberta agreed. She felt we had been through enough and did not need to be around for the final exiting of Jeanette, though she did not anticipate that it would be difficult. She said she simply wanted to be able to concentrate fully to be sure everything was conveyed in a way that Jeanette could accept.

It was another week before Roberta could come to Carlston, but that was OK. Now that we had a date, we settled in to work and write and get caught up on everything. Peter was back on the job and doing as well as ever. His vacation had been everything he was hoping for, including a chance encounter with the girl of his dreams. She was Peter's first love, and our young employee, we were told by his parents, walked around with the kind of expression you see only on the newly in bliss. It was great to hear the energy in his voice, and we congratulated ourselves, once again, for having hired him.

In fact, having Peter working for us completely changed the way I did business. Instead of traveling every week, as I had done for years and assumed I would do forever, I now was planning to travel about once a month for just a few days.

I called a travel agent and made reservations for Anna and me to depart for Phoenix the day after Roberta would arrive at our house.

From there we would rent a car and head north to Sedona. I was armed with brochures from the travel agency, and a list of hotels from the Internet, as we drove out to the Dunes for supper.

It wasn't the first time we had been back since the incident over the pie safe, but it was the first time we'd been back since we came home from Florida. We had answers now, and Anna was seriously uninterested in talking about Jeanette anymore. So Gina couldn't have been more off the money when she greeted us with her usual hugs and made Anna an offer she couldn't wait to refuse.

"Honey, I've been thinking about that old pie safe," Gina started. She had this way of very gently pushing Anna's hair back from her face like a mother might do when she wants to talk about something serious. Then she rested her hands on Anna's shoulders. "If it came from your house in the first place, I think maybe you should have it back. I really don't think it's right for me to have it here, and I told you I didn't pay much for it. I'll find something else to hold these old dishes. I'd like to give it to you, honey. We'll call it a birthday present."

Anna was startled by the unexpected offer, and I could tell immediately that the pie safe was the last thing she wanted in our house. She was starting to pale out, and I got ready to move in if needed.

"Oh, Gina, that is so sweet of you . . ." she said, stepping back slightly. "I really appreciate your offer, but you were so excited when you got it, and I think it belongs here. If it sits in our house, the only people who will ever see it are our few guests, but here, it's going to be enjoyed by all your customers every day. It's been put to really good use here, Gina, and it fits. It should stay. Thank you so much, but please, let's keep it here."

I think Gina didn't really want to part with it, and she was happy to accept Anna's refusal.

Twenty minutes after we got home, the phone rang, and Anna picked it up.

&. *"Hey, Annie, it's me, Janice."*

Of course. I expected the call. John was too much of a cash cow for her to leave him alone.

"Hello, Janice. How's everything?" I wasn't caught completely off guard, but I sure didn't know what to say to her.

"We're good here, Louie and me. Glad we reached you. I thought I remembered John saying you lived in Michigan in some city that started with a C. I found you through the Internet on the computer at the library."

Lucky us. "John's upstairs," I told her. "I'll call him."

I held the cordless phone against my sweater and walked up to John's office, where he was poring over a new catalog from a nursery that specialized in plants for shade gardens.

"It's for you, John. It's Janice."

John looked up at me like I had just made a bad joke and asked if I was kidding. I shook my head from side to side and handed him the phone. Then I took a seat in the corner. He just kept looking at me, while a thousand questions passed across his face. I smiled and pantomimed that he should put the phone up to his mouth and say hello.

"Hello, Janice . . . We're good, thanks, and you?"

John was silent for a few moments, and I guessed that Janice was telling him just how good she was. In a smooth move, he reached for the handset of the phone on his desk, pushed the speaker button and turned off the cordless extension.

". . . and we think you may have gotten the wrong impression of us, little brother. See, Louie was a bit nervous about people coming in the house, because like I told you, he was accused of a little crime over at one of the grocery stores in town. So he's been keeping that gun around just to sort of scare off people he don't know. I don't think he even knows how to use it, do you, Louie!"

I heard her chuckle at that, as though the thought of Louie using a gun was just too funny.

"Jeez, Johnnie, he didn't mean to scare *you*. You know, nearly everyone down here has a gun now. We don't keep it loaded. It's just more or less like something to wave around in case the situation gets a little unfriendly. Anyway, Louie is real sorry that he was sleeping while you were here, because he'd like to meet you, and we thought that we might come on up and see you and stay a while. Louie is from Alabama, and he's never been much further north than the Mason-Dixon Line. It always sort of scared him, you know. People down here got funny ideas about the North. I mean, really, Johnnie, you think Louie scared you? Well, you ought to see what happens down here when you tell people you got relatives in Michigan. They think it's nothing but snow and mosquitoes and liberals, and they wouldn't be caught dead going up there. I usually make a little joke and tell them that they won't be caught dead because there's no death penalty, and then they really get nervous. Anyway, Johnnie, I been telling Louie about how pretty Michigan is because you got all those lakes and all. And so we thought we'd throw some stuff in the car and head on up to see you. What do you say, Johnnie? First impressions aren't everything. Will you give us another chance?"

~ *A deer in the headlights—that's what I'm sure I looked like. I was* stunned. Anna saw this coming, but I sure didn't.

"How long do you think you'd be staying, Janice?"

"Well, we're moving out of this place in a week or so, and we got nothing holding us here, so we were thinking maybe we'd stay with you until we get on our feet, and then we'll look for a place of our own."

"In Michigan?"

"Yeah, maybe even Carlston. I figure you've got some friends there who might be able to help Louie get a job."

My heart started pounding.

"Janice, I'm sorry, but I don't think that will work."

Silence.

"Are you there?" I asked.

"Yeah, I'm here."

I stumbled ahead.

"Janice, just a couple weeks ago, you were happy to be living in Florida and smoking pot and eager to get whatever Pete had stored away for you in the drawer which I can only assume was something not legal. And you seemed quite comfortable having an unemployed boyfriend sleeping on the couch with a gun resting on his stomach. I don't want any part of that life. My guess is that you're leaving the state because you have to, for whatever reason, and you're coming here to hide. I can't help you."

"Will you just get off your high horse for one minute, John? Don't you think you owe me a little consideration, given that you're up there in Michigan living like a king and I'm here in a rented house that's falling down, and trying to make ends meet with a disability check? Isn't it about time you become the brother—the man—that Mom and

Dad hoped you'd be and extend your hand to your sister when she's down on her luck? Don't you remember how I always used to take care of you when you were little . . ."

"Janice, stop." I would rather have been eating furniture glue than have this conversation. I was no good at this. I barely knew this woman anymore, yet everything she said was true. Brother. Sister. She, struggling. He, stable and happy. Part of me felt so guilty. Then I looked at Anna sitting in the corner.

"You made choices to get to this point. I am not responsible for your choices, and it's not my job to get you out of trouble. You can't just change geography and expect that your life will suddenly right itself, Janice. Coming to Michigan isn't going to solve anything for you . . . Anna and I are not running a halfway house." I regretted that last comment as soon as it came out of my mouth. It was unnecessary. There was more silence.

"Johnnie, you're all I got left."

I couldn't tell if she was slurring or starting to cry.

"That's not true, honey. You have that wonderful mind you were born with. I'm sorry, Janice. I really am sorry, but I can't help you. I'd like to, but I can't. Not here in Carlston. I think you need some counseling and probably another visit to a treatment center. If you want, I'll help you find a place where you can go. I can do some research and see what I can come up with. I'll make some calls. And I think we can help you pay for it. But at some point, Janice, you need to realize that you're living a dead-end life the way you're going."

I was struggling to find the right words, and these weren't it. I was pretty sure she would start to argue with me again, which had always been her style, so I thought I'd get another chance to make more sense.

But there was silence on her end. Then a quiet, trembling sigh.

"Yeah, baby brother. That sounds good. I'll think about that." Her voice was flat and detached. I know this was not how she had intended the conversation to go. I knew I was losing her. I heard Louie say "here" like he had handed her something.

"Janice, when you get resettled, give me a call again, and let me know how you're doing. OK?"

"Yeah, Johnnie. I'll do that."

I said good-bye, but she had already hung up.

🕭 *John and I have learned that ghosts take many forms. Sometimes they are* unrested spirits like Jeanette—people who can't leave the present until they have resolved the past. They have deep, personal and sometimes terrifying issues, and unwittingly, we walk into their complex world. We are not so much a target as a vehicle for them to express themselves and expunge whatever tenuous threads hold them here.

Sometimes ghosts are people who are still very much alive and who have a troubled past that is woven tightly with our own—a parent, a child, a first love. This was the case with Janice. After years of no communication, she lingered like a persistent fog in John's head, a skinny, weather-beaten apparition who was damaged by her dysfunctional parents, who did damage to them in return and who disappeared into a living limbo called Tampa.

Had John not decided to try to find Janice when we were visiting Mike, I believe she would have surfaced at another time, and John would have had to deal, then, with all the issues between them. That she and Mike both lived in Tampa . . . and that Mike and John were both in search of sisters. . . . well, those were pretty amazing coincidences.

Mostly, this is my point. Some ghosts pass through walls to get to us. Others, like Janice, simply stand at an open door and welcome us in.

Wednesday morning I awoke with a terrible headache and a temperature of 101. John freaked, and I wondered if I would ever again be able to get sick without both of us assuming I was *possessed*. God, I hate that word. Anyway, it was cold and snowy out, and the thought of staying in bed with a pot of tea and a book on Arizona hiking trails that John had picked up for us—well, it seemed a wonderful way to pass the morning. I took some aspirin and settled in. I remember asking for some soup around noon. John told me he brought it up perhaps fifteen minutes later, along with some toast and a slice of pound cake. But I had fallen asleep again, and he decided I needed rest more than food.

I awoke around four o'clock p.m. and rolled over to look out the windows. Even in the dusky low winter light, I could see that it had started snowing hard. The wind was gusting, as well, and it felt like the temperature—in the house—had dropped. That was easy to explain. Many of our windows were still nothing more than wavy single panes of glass installed when dirt was new, and they were loose in their frames to boot. Chasing a ghost had distracted us from the business of renovating—imagine that—and with a good east wind going, we sometimes awoke to tiny snow piles around the edges of the sashes.

Once, we opened a portion of an exterior wall to install a new window and discovered it had been packed tight as a sausage with spruce cones and walnut shells—the work of incredibly industrious squirrels. We thought about keeping all that decades-old stuff right where we found it, as it was the only evidence of insulation we could find.

And we've already mentioned the inefficiency of our old and not-so-trusty furnace, which we had not yet replaced. Despite John's observation on our first walk through of the house that hot July morning when he declared that the furnace had probably seen its last winter, it was still with us.

I chuckled a bit, thinking about how long we had lived with our bulbous monster. We had even given it a name, Old Torrid, taken from the words on its cast-iron loading door, Torrid Zone. We discovered during our first winter with it that the furnace's pilot light (remember those?) had a disconcerting habit of going out when the wind blew stronger than thirty miles per hour. And here along the lakeshore, that happens a lot. Last spring, we decided to shut off the gas to the furnace and keep it off all summer. That saved us some money and gave us peace of mind.

Because the furnace was old, and frankly, because it looked like a lot of people who weren't furnace experts had made modifications to it over time, describing it as not being in great shape is a huge understatement. Still, it had huffed its way through our first winter and was huffing its way through this one too, and I had learned the delicate art of relighting the pilot, which came in very handy when John was traveling.

About a week after returning from Florida, we had come home from a long day of doing errands and found the house nearly as cold inside as outside. We knew immediately that the pilot light had failed again. We got it lit, and John called the furnace guy, who had become nearly our best friend on the strength of broken-furnace visits alone. He arrived a few hours later and verified that the aging thermocouple was at fault. And oh, by the way, the heat exchanger was on the brink of failure as well.

Fortunately, he did not red-tag us, which means he would have felt we were in sufficient danger of being gassed to death that he would

145

have disconnected the furnace from the gas source so we could not use it. He did some quick tests on the ambient air quality in the house and did not detect high amounts of carbon monoxide or anything else deadly to cause alarm. He knew there was a waiting list for furnace installations this time of year, and that in the interim, if he condemned our furnace, we would have to move out, and the house would freeze and the pipes would burst.

Instead, he called his office to check the earliest opening when they could put in a new unit. Because we did have a mostly working furnace, compared to people whose primary heat source was completely dead, we were not put on the urgent list. And that was OK. We set a date.

Old Torrid was finally seeing its last winter.

Recalling this makes us sound pretty negligent. All winter long we had heard the volunteer fire department alarm go off, and we had read about houses catching fire because of faulty furnaces, but I guess we thought we were immune. And in our defense, we were focused on other priorities. But now that we had finally made a commitment to get the work done, we were ready and eager. When I came downstairs around five Wednesday evening and mentioned that I was chilly, John realized he had been so engrossed in a basketball game on TV that he had failed to notice the dropping temperature inside.

~ *OK, I felt very stupid. Months earlier, at the beginning of the winter, when* it took the repairman two hours to get the furnace fired up and running properly, I should have simply suggested that we chuck Old Torrid then. But instead, here we were, in the middle of a blizzard, with my wife sick in bed, and I get so stuck on a game that I don't realize it's fifty-eight degrees inside. Well, the new furnace was scheduled to be installed the next day, and this would be the last night I would lie in bed wondering if the clanking in the basement meant that in an hour or two I would have to get up and go light the pilot one more time.

I headed downstairs with a box of matches, only to be greeted by a mess. Broken wine bottles again. It seemed that the storage area in the crawl space that I thought would be so perfect for stacking wine crates shifted with every change of season, and when that happened, invariably a bottle or three slipped out of the cubbies and went sailing to the basement floor. Which, you will recall, was concrete. Have you ever broken a bottle of wine on concrete? How about three bottles? It's a mushy, splintery, dangerous mess. I think something happens to wine when it leaves the bottle. Pour it in a glass or two, and it disappears remarkably quickly, but spill it out on the floor and I swear it doubles in volume. My mother used to say the same thing about a glass of milk or juice that got knocked off the kitchen table. It runs everywhere. So, once again, I got out the dustpan, which I now kept handy, and went in search of some rags. I was getting tired of this. I don't know if I was more frustrated by letting the house get cold, by not getting the furnace fixed the year before or by losing another couple bottles of wine. But I'll tell you, I wasn't a happy guy.

About ten minutes into the project, I was startled by the sound of the furnace firing up. I had been so sidetracked getting the wine and glass cleaned up that I had forgotten to relight the pilot. When the furnace kicked on, I realized the pilot wasn't out. Swell. That meant that other parts of the furnace were starting to malfunction. Or maybe the thermostat was getting wonky, and that was why the heat didn't go on. Then I realized none of that mattered. In less than twenty-four hours, Old Torrid would be history. I congratulated myself on having finally scheduled installation of the new furnace. Clearly, it was not a moment too soon. Anna and I could toss some extra quilts on the bed in case the fire went out again, and we'd be fine until tomorrow.

Anna made corn chowder for supper. The wind was howling, and it tasted good. We ate it with some bread I had made the day before—my first attempt at baking, and it wasn't bad. Flour, water, salt, oil, yeast. Simple.

Thursday morning the heating guys arrived right on schedule and headed downstairs to remove the old furnace. We had always assumed it was installed when the house was built, maybe put in when the foundation was laid, so the house could be built up and over it. Or it could have been installed by hauling it in through the old coal doors. We didn't know how it got there, but we knew how it wasn't getting out. The coal doors had long been bricked over, and the "new" stairway that went up into the kitchen wasn't wide enough or straight enough to allow the furnace to be carried out that way. So the technicians went to work on Old Torrid using a couple of sledgehammers to crack its iron shell. I don't know what their hearing was like when they were through, but the whole house was ringing from two hours of pounding on our defenseless furnace. It seemed a terribly unjust ending for a piece of equipment that had unfailingly—well, almost unfailingly—served so many families and kept the house warm through so many decades of blizzards and winter storms. In fact, it was damn depressing. And, I might add, it was cold.

Having no heat while the guys worked to break up and haul out the old unit piece by piece, and then haul in the new unit and install it, meant the house started drifting into the upper fifties by late afternoon. Bundled in long johns and a sweater, I watched while the new Amana, tiny compared to its predecessor, was uncrated. I was relieved that it could be easily carried down the stairs. It occupied less than a quarter of the footprint of Old Torrid, and without anticipating it, we gained several square feet of storage space in the basement.

❧ *I was feeling good on Thursday until the pounding started. That was at* about nine a.m. John said that hearing the old furnace get beaten to pieces upset him, and I agreed. In fact, I wanted to get out of the house, because I just couldn't stand the noise and the sadness of it.

I don't think John mentioned that at dawn that morning—I had been thinking about this most of the night—I suggested he move all the wine out of the crawl space so the concussion from pounding on Old Torrid didn't jar the wooden cases and knock the remaining wine bottles to the floor. We had a bountiful supply, but lately we were losing wine at the rate of one or two bottles each week, and that was going to seriously dent our supply if it kept up. Before the workers arrived, John went downstairs and moved every stinking case—there were about twenty—to the other side of the basement. It was a good plan. I can't imagine they would have stood still, literally, for the vibrations of the sledgehammer blows just a few feet away.

I headed to the grocery store with a long list, since Roberta was due to arrive Friday afternoon. She said she would get to our house around four p.m., after she got her second-shift staff checked in at the café, and after she finished payroll. I was so grateful that she was carving out some time for us. John and I knew she was very busy. The café was now featuring live music in the evenings, and though it stopped serving full meals around three p.m., it was doing a brisk tavern business since Roberta had obtained a beer and wine license and put together evening offerings that included coffee, tea, juice, appetizers and desserts, plus organic beers and wines. The food and drinks buoyed the book business, and vice-versa.

We thought it was a brilliant move, but characteristically, Roberta took little credit. She said she simply sat down one day to try to figure out what her most inspiring, restful, contented evening would look like, and then replicated that image in her café. What she loved was a comfortable chair, a glass of wine, something decadent to eat and soft live music in the background. And no surprise, she discovered that she wasn't the only one who sought that combination.

Gentle and warm as she was, Roberta was a shrewd business-woman. Her staff was well trained, and they performed well or were dismissed. I don't think she was ever mean or unfair. She just knew what she wanted, and what her customers deserved. She was firm, convincing and unwilling to settle for less than excellence, whether it was the food, the service, the music or the products she sold. Even the attitude of her staff was measured regularly and fine-tuned when necessary. In return, she told us, she paid her workers more than the going rate and gave generous vacation and personal leave. I'll tell you, her diligence made a difference. Going there was always a joy. Her cooks, waitstaff and salespeople seemed happy and well cared for, and thus, so were her customers.

Though we were leaving for Arizona on Saturday, I wanted to stock the house with things for Roberta to eat while she was there. John had added a few things to the list as well. It was a relief to be away from the noise at home. Lately, with the breaking wine bottles and furnace problems, and the still-unresolved issue of Jeanette's unwelcome presence, I was wishing we had bought the brand-new condo one block from Lake Michigan that we had passed up in favor of Maple Hill. Hindsight is so unfair.

Anyway, I wandered through the produce department, loading up on stuff for a hearty winter soup, thinking that would be something I could make Friday morning and heat up when Roberta arrived. I knew the house would be dependably toasty once the new furnace was finally turned on, but since we had returned from Florida, I just couldn't seem to get warm. Running from the car to the grocery store, I could feel the cold right through my layers of sweatshirt, fleece, and jacket. Even in a flannel nightgown and socks, and with my thickest comforter piled on, I had been waking up cold most nights.

John asked me to go to the health food store and see if I could find something called spelt that he needed for a loaf of bread he wanted to make. He had found the recipe in my old *Companion* cookbook and thought it sounded interesting. He also wanted to try making corn pudding. I wasn't sure when he would find the time to fit all this industrious baking in between tonight and tomorrow afternoon, nor was I sure when we would eat it, but I wasn't going to discourage him, since this was the first real interest he had shown in cooking in months. And having the oven on helped heat the kitchen.

I hoped Roberta would bring a few of her pumpkin muffins. That would take care of breakfast on Saturday, and by eleven a.m., we would be on our way to the airport. All that was left to find was a pretty clutch of fresh flowers—no easy task in a small town in the middle of winter. I wanted to make up a small vase for the dresser in Roberta's bedroom.

Before John and I made our reservations for the Southwest, we had asked Roberta how long she would be at our house. She was pretty vague, and I didn't press. She said she didn't know how long it would take her to connect with Jeanette. It wasn't, after all, like picking up the phone and making a long-distance call. It could take a few days, she explained. Or just a few minutes. It all depended on a lot of things that John and I didn't understand and, frankly, we didn't want to understand. So, we planned to fly back home the following Friday, which felt like a good amount of time for us to be able to see all that Sedona had to offer, and to take a day trip or two into the surrounding countryside. We had tickets for a train ride to the Grand Canyon and reservations for one night at a huge old log lodge along the canyon rim. Except for that and a few local tours, we didn't plan to push the tourist stuff. Our goal was to relax, drink good coffee, be awed by the red rocks and relax some more. Oh yeah ... and I really was hoping to have a psychic reading. Can you believe it?

By the time I arrived home from the store, the new furnace was cranking out the BTUs and attempting to spread warmth to every corner of our chilly house. I say "attempting" because it seemed to be taking a long time to do so. We surmised it was because the house had been cold for so long, or because we were now heating absolutely every cubic inch. The furnace guys had recommended installing some new ductwork in rooms that were previously unheated, like the bathrooms on both floors and a guestroom that we never used. They added some new cold air returns as well. Having a house with even temperature top to bottom was, for us, a luxury beyond comprehension, but we thought it prudent to follow their recommendation.

While the furnace itself was nearly silent, the fan was another matter. There was now a sizeable volume of air moving throughout the house. The old furnace had a blower, but it was ancient and not very powerful. By contrast, this furnace was making dust balls swirl around on the floor. The new setup would take some getting used to.

John was happy to see that I had found spelt. He wanted to get going on the bread recipe and had begun preheating the oven hours before the dough would be ready to bake.

Before the furnace techs left, John talked with them about the problem we were having with the shifting wine crates, and they suggested it was probably due to the frequent swings of extreme temperatures in the basement. When the pilot went out, it got very cold down there. When the furnace was back on, the basement got very warm, because the old furnace didn't have a lick of insulation, and it had to burn for hours to raise the temperature upstairs to something close to livable. Satisfied with their logic, and knowing that the new furnace would provide a much more even basement temperature, John moved all the wine crates back to the crawl space and reorganized the bottles according to type, rather than brand. It was something he'd wanted to do for a while.

It was only when he was talking with the installers that he realized the extremes in temperatures that caused the ground to shift were probably also deteriorating the wine. The cold wasn't so much of a problem, because it never went below freezing in the basement, but heat is an enemy of wine. Funny that we hadn't thought of that earlier, but we really spent very little time in the basement, and since we went down there mostly to relight the pilot, it was usually cold. And it was always cool in summer. We never thought about how warm it might get down there when the furnace was on. Oh well. Water over the dam, or wine over the wall, as we had grown fond of saying. Most of the contents of the cellar had come to us as gifts from grateful vintners. It was a good collection, but mostly free, and replaceable.

As his final act of wine cellar management that evening, John marked each of the bottles with a yellow tag, signaling that they had been exposed to the temperature fluctuations and therefore should be the first bottles consumed. Then he grabbed a bottle of Chateau Nevermore to go with the sweet potato soup I was making for supper.

~ *When Anna and I crawled into bed that night, it felt surprisingly good* knowing that probably not again in my lifetime would I have to worry about waking in the middle of the night to a frigid house and a fume-spewing furnace.

We had gotten used to keeping our thermostat set at around sixty-five degrees during the day and dressing in layers to stay warm. Because the wind outside was bitter, we decided to keep the heat up on that first night of new-furnace luxury instead of turning it down to our usual choice of a bracing fifty-five degrees. The HVAC guys had installed a programmable thermostat that we could set to automatically drop to a lower temperature as we were going to bed, and to go back up about a half hour before our alarm went off. It was a brilliant invention.

I don't think I would have made it in the early part of the century, when outhouses were still in use in our tiny town, and one's ability to heat a dwelling was measured by one's access to wood and one's skill with an ax. There was one thing I envied about guys back then, however. They got to grow beards, and nobody raised an eyebrow. In fact, at times, they were thought to be a practical fashion, and were a sign of manliness—at least to other men. Anna knew I was tired of shaving every day, so she wasn't surprised when she rolled over to kiss me good night and found herself face-to-face with stubble.

"Did you decide to stop shaving, honey?" she asked tactfully.

"Yeah. It's freezing out, and it doesn't make sense to me that I go out and buy expensive clothing to stay warm and then deliberately shave off this free insulation on my face. Do you mind?"

"It fits you," she replied, and then added, "I'm doing the same thing with the hair on my legs."

&♣ *On Friday morning, I crawled out of bed, wrapped my comforter around* me and headed for the warmth of a shower. The house should have been warm. The new furnace had been working all night, and despite the fact that it was a chilly twenty-four degrees outside, we assumed that the inside of the house should have warmed up to greater than sixty-three degrees. We couldn't seem to get it past that point. I fiddled around with the new thermostat to see if John had programmed it incorrectly.

By now you know that John and I are not techo-wizards by any stretch. But they sell these things to ordinary citizens, and we thought anybody with a third-grade education ought to be able to make it run. We decided that if the temperature didn't go up substantially by noon, we would call the furnace company and have them come back and take a look. I made a quick run again to the grocery for a few things I had forgotten. I was wearing a long skirt, heavy leggings and work boots. Must have been an interesting look.

At four o'clock the phone rang. It was Roberta. She was heading out the door of the café. Everything there was peaceable and under control, she told me. The staff was doing their usual good job. A big shipment of food for the weekend had come, and everything was already put away. The entertainment had been confirmed, and Roberta was free to head to Carlston. She thought she would arrive about 5:30.

Despite my eager anticipation of seeing Roberta, my stomach was churning. I decided my anxiety was completely normal, given the purpose of Roberta's visit. But in the back of my mind . . . no, really, it was in the very front of my mind . . . were these really horrible thoughts. . . . What if all we had done wasn't good enough for Jeanette? What if we had headed down the wrong path and found the wrong person? What if Jeanette declined to leave?

John was cooking up a storm. I wasn't quite sure about the growth on his chin. It was at the point where he just looked shady—like a guy who got lost on a barroom floor for a while. But he was happy about his fledgling beard, so I kept quiet. I did wonder if it would get a rise out of Roberta.

At 5:30 almost on the nose, the kitchen door opened, and in walked our darling friend. My very first thought was that she looked different. Thinner maybe. And drawn. I would have thought that her travels to New Mexico would have given her a bit of a tan, but she was pale. Her hair was long and loose. And she looked tired. In fact, I had never seen such a look on her face. John and I had often remarked that Roberta seemed to have more energy than any three people we knew. She never, ever, even with long hours at the café, talked about being weary or worn-out or any of those words most of us use at some point. But the expression on her face—the lines and the fatigue that I saw in her eyes—was so pronounced that I had to work to not register my shock. Even the way she hugged was different. Through all our time together, I had come to know Roberta as open and loving. There was never that superficial pat-pat-pat on the back that people are most comfortable with. Her embrace had been warm and sweet and honest from the first day we met. Until now.

~ *While we waited for Roberta to arrive, I had decided to do a little* cooking. Anna had gone to the store in the morning, so I had tied on an apron and sat down with Anna's vintage cookbook to see what sounded good for supper. I had already planned to make a couple soups, and Anna had picked up raisins so I could make a dark brown bread, thick with molasses and oats. It sounded like someone's old family recipe. Like Anna, I was nervous about Roberta coming back, but I was easily preoccupied by my newfound interest in cooking. And by the way, the garden catalogs were starting to pile up in the parlor, and I found few things more satisfying than sitting down with a cup of tea and poring through them to see what was new and what we might have fun trying when the weather broke and the ground could be made ready to plant again.

I wanted an herb garden out the back door, and I planned to add to Anna's rose garden.

I turned to watch CNN for a few minutes on a small television in the corner of the kitchen. Anna had been cleaning in anticipation of Roberta's arrival, and I assumed she had moved the TV table a bit as it was no longer square to the corner, so I moved it back into its place. Just as I was settling back in to catch the sports report, I caught a whiff of the bread I was baking. Apparently, I had not heard the timer buzz, but all was well. The bread was fine—puffy and golden—and it filled the kitchen with a wonderful fragrance.

The one thing I wanted to do before Roberta arrived was go to the basement and pull a few bottles of wine as gifts for her. We had come to know her taste in reds, and I thought if there was time that evening, we would introduce her to Mike's fabulous sangria. I had hoped to insulate the door between the furnace and the wine room before we left for Arizona. The new furnace was insulated and not likely to cause the temperature fluctuation we had experienced with Old Torrid, but I felt that insulating the door would be one more measure to protect our dwindling wine supply and assure a more constant cavelike temperature for it.

You might think after all that had taken place, Anna and I would have packed our suitcases months ago and run screaming from this nutty place. But aside from the drama with Jeanette, we had come to love our old house. It had been incredibly affordable, which would make it possible for us to slow down and take some time off work. We had a small manageable monthly mortgage payment that we could make even with my reduced hours and if Anna chose to not work at all. We loved Maple Hill with its big old rooms and peeling paper and squeaky floorboards and even the drafty old wavy glass windows. I knew if we chose to stay in the house, we would replace those windows over the next few years, and eventually replace crumbling plaster and pre-code electrical wiring. For me, the windows would be last. So many people had looked through them and watched this town change over the decades. We'd have to find something productive to do with them . . . perhaps cobble together a small greenhouse or storm porch. It would be unthinkable to simply yank them out and drop them at the dump.

Our search had been so focused on Martin and Jeanette since we moved in that we had never had time to research any of the families that lived here after them. I wondered about the children who had slid down the railing on their bottoms from the second floor, just as I had done as a child in my grandparents' house. I wondered what Christmas mornings had been like there, the beautiful trees that had brightened the corners of the rooms, the lean years during depressions, the tears shed when jobs were lost and bank accounts emptied and the bountiful years when the harvest was celebrated and meals were shared with family and friends.

I thought of the footsteps and laughter of children that once rang through this house, the games in the yard, the dogs that had slept at the foot of their owners' beds, the cats in the windowsills and even the chickens that had probably dashed around the yard and the old barn, now turned garage.

I thought about the war years and the memorials in town to the young men from this area who had lost their lives during two world wars. I wondered if any had lived in this house. There is also a tiny monument to those who fought and died in Korea, and a very living tribute to Vietnam veterans that you can see any Friday night at the VFW fish fry. There are usually several men dressed in fatigues, wrinkles at the corners of their eyes, a cigarette and drink in hand. They are our very own heroes who fought an unwinnable war and came back to a country united only in its anger, so preoccupied by protest that we could not keep separate our disdain for the war and our support for the soldiers.

Anna and I lost a friend a few years ago to alcoholism. He had been a star in his high school class—a role model—who came back from Vietnam and was slowly devoured by the memory of his experiences. The war in Iraq had brought it all back and tipped him over the edge. He slipped away one quiet evening surrounded by empty bottles.

Anna wrote an article for our local paper called the "Uncounted Casualties of War" in which she profiled two veterans, our friend and a local woman who had also served in Vietnam. Both escaped injury but died on their native soil years later from deep, decades-old, bloodless wounds. I thought the article was one of Anna's best.

I digress, but those were the thoughts that were going through my head that Friday afternoon as I waited for Roberta. I knew that once this business with Jeanette was settled and we put it behind us, Anna and I would have fun searching through the county books and libraries to get some of the other history on this house. I wanted to know who else had walked these buttery oak floors.

By noon the temp was up to sixty-nine inside, and I knew we were finally on the right track with the thermostat. Though even at that, the house felt chilly. The long underwear I had on helped. I threw a cardigan over my apron, and decided that the strain of the last several months had had an effect on my health, too. Stress, you know, can make people sick.

I had the same reaction as Anna when Roberta walked in the door. She looked strained. I wondered what it must be like living alone and running a business alone, and having no one to come home to at the end of a busy day. But if her hug was cool, I did not notice. I was just relieved to see her.

Distracted by my baking earlier, I hadn't yet fetched any wine, so while Roberta and Anna got caught up on family news, I headed to the basement.

The cold air hit me as soon as I opened the door, and for a moment,

156

I anticipated having to light the old pilot again. Then I chuckled at what a creature of habit I had become, and how good it was to remember that we had a new furnace. A new $6,500 furnace. State of the art. Stop worrying, I told myself. Still, the steps felt icy, and I could see my breath. The handrail was white and slick, like a tree branch covered with hoarfrost. The air stung my nose. And there was the unmistakable sound of a wine bottle crashing to the cement floor. I started to swear before I reached the bottom step. The hair was up on the back of my neck, and every inch of skin tingled. When I turned the corner into the wine room, I knew we had big trouble. The floor was covered with broken glass and wine, and bottles were slipping out of the crates like salmon going over rapids. I shouted for Anna and spread my arms across the wine crates, trying to stop the chaos, but my reach was short and bottles slid out above and below my arms as though they were programmed to self-destruct.

Anna was at the door of the room in seconds, then stopped abruptly—hands to her mouth. Her eyes got big and rolled slowly from side to side, trying, I assumed, to make sense of the bizarre scene in front of her.

"Help me pull these crates," I shouted, hoping she could navigate the floor and remove some of the wine that remained. But the only part of her that moved was her eyes.

"Anna!" I shouted again, trying to get her focused on the task at hand. "Grab the wine bottles!" But there was no reaction from her.

Roberta followed on the steps behind her, then came around to her side and tried to direct Anna back upstairs. I thought she was concerned that Anna was going into shock.

"We need to get her out of here, John," she said, taking Anna by the arm to turn her, but Anna, suddenly animated, shook off Roberta and started walking toward the crates, to my great relief. I turned away to try to catch another bottle and heard thunder vibrate through the foundation, followed by an ear-shattering explosion of wood and glass. Anna had calmly wrapped her arms around a full crate of wine from the still-intact stack and sent it to the basement floor.

"What the hell?" I yelled.

"Get her out of here, John," Roberta yelled. "Let me take care of this. Get Anna out of here."

I was distracted by Roberta just long enough for Anna to methodically pull a second case of bottles from the stack. Then a third and a fourth and a fifth. Pull, crash. Pull, crash. Pull, crash. The stench of spilled wine and alcohol fumes were making me dizzy, and the noise . . . it was so loud it hurt.

I tried to get to Anna, but we were both shin deep in slippery broken glass and splintered wood crates, and I was struggling just to keep my footing. I knew if I fell, I could be sliced in a hundred places and bleed to death in minutes. All I could do was shout. Roberta was heading for Anna, just as the thunder came trembling through the foundation again, rolling waves of it, like an earthquake, that shook more bottles to the floor. And then a voice.

Dig.

Roberta reached up to grab a beam. She was pale.

Deeper.

It was loud, even louder than the still crashing wine crates. Audible even above the thunder.

Dig. Deeper. Dig DEEPER DIG DEEPER DIG DEEPER.

In less than twenty seconds, Anna had dumped every single remaining crate and bottle, and the voice changed. It was softer.

Dig deeper. Over and over. Breathy. The same meaningless command I had heard in the hospital so many months earlier. But gentle now. Fading in and out. Not demanding. Pleading.

I stood helpless and knew that Anna belonged for the moment to someone else. Roberta was still calling to her, but deaf to both of us, Anna stretched her arms out over the crawl space in front of her, cupped her hands and began digging, eyes closed, mouth moving but making no sound. She dragged loads of powdery soil to the edge of the old knee wall and sent it, like the wine bottles, to the basement floor.

Then, abruptly, she stopped. And the thunder was quiet, and the voice was silent.

Roberta reached for Anna again, and then backed off suddenly, as though she had been slapped. Slowly, very slowly, Anna reached into the crater she had created, and with only a little difficulty, dislodged a wooden box. A tattered fruit label was still glued to the outside. She pressed it to her chest and turned to me, her arms dusted with sand, her giant blue eyes filling with tears.

"Anna, give me the box, and let's get you out of here," Roberta began, holding out her hand. "Come here, honey. Let me take that for you."

I don't believe Anna even heard her. She shifted the box so she could cradle it securely with one arm, brushed the loose dirt from the top and slowly lifted the lid.

I had never given thought to what the body of a six-month-old child would look like after being buried for ninety years. Still, I knew immediately that we had finally found Rose. Her wool sweater with those telltale tiny pearl buttons that we had seen in the photos was still wrapped around her little skeleton, dark curls poking out from under a yellowing bonnet. Baby Rose. Dead at six months, buried in secret, her remains now resting in a box in Anna's arms. I turned away, suddenly sick to my stomach.

❧ *No, I wasn't horrified, just very sad. Nobody had to tell me it was Rose. I* knew it as soon as I started digging. And yes, I do remember digging. I remember pains shooting up my arms, and I remember closing my eyes and seeing the whole story then—Jeanette sick and weeping, searching for something that could serve as a casket for her tiny daughter, and the wooden crate she took from the attic, which had once been packed with dishes—a gift from the nuns.

Mostly, I remember the sadness. I felt it deeply—the kind of sadness that drives you to solitude because even the smallest hint of compassion feels like a mockery of your pain. I felt it.

And then, bleeding and reeking of wine and sweat, after months of searching for answers to an abduction that never happened . . . I got mad. I put the top back on the box, turned and handed it to Roberta to take upstairs, knowing she would make sense of it for us later. She reached for the box, bowed her head and backed out of the chaos.

I was touched by the thought that this basement had served as a burial ground for this poor child. But mostly, I was furious that we had been led on a completely unnecessary search for this very baby who was never more than one hundred feet from us in this house. Jeanette's antics had cost us a lot of time and money, strained our marriage and nearly killed me.

I was scared and exhausted and angry, and I started yelling. "She lied to us. She lied to us . . . she LIED to us!!!"

I made a fist and pounded the knee wall. "She lied to us!"

I stomped my feet on the broken glass heaped around me. "She LIED to us!"

I reached up and slammed my hands on the beams. "She LIED to us!" I yelled as loud as I could, over and over, five, six, seven more times. "She LIED to us! She LIED to us!" And then I stood absolutely still, thinking that Jeanette might have something to say. An apology perhaps. Or another lie?

The silence made me even angrier.

John had stopped retching and was leaning against the wall, looking a fine shade of gray, shaking his head slowly. I could only imagine his thoughts . . . his wife was losing her mind . . . his wine collection lay shattered at his feet . . . and the corpse of an infant in a wooden box had just been carried up to his kitchen.

"It's over, Anna. It's over." John's voice was alarmingly quiet. "Pick your way out of this mess, and go upstairs. Ask Roberta to take a look at the cuts on your arms. I'll be up in a minute."

Oh, God. . . . Roberta. I had forgotten about her as soon as I handed her the box. She would be devastated by this. "She lied, John," I said once more. "Jeanette lied to us."

John took a deep breath as the furnace kicked on. "Yeah, I know she did."

No," said a thin voice behind me. "*I* lied."

Epilogue

~ *On Saturday morning, Anna and I got up before dawn, canceled our* airline tickets and made a list of everything we needed to do that day. Mike had been on our minds all night. We were concerned about the impact that our news of finding Rose's body would have on him, so we decided to call him after dinner that evening when we could relax a bit and give him our full attention. In retrospect, we needn't have worried. Mike was saddened but philosophical about losing what had seemed a pretty clear link to Mary's origins. He was happy that our drama was finally resolved and as shocked as we by the violent finale. Most surprising, Mike asked if he could come visit us in June. He had enjoyed our week together in Florida and felt a friendship growing between us. We were touched and agreed.

At ten a.m., after delivering to the county coroner the wooden box holding Rose's remains, we headed to Grand Rapids. A shoebox between us held a bag of chocolate chip cookies, some photos of the house taken when we first moved in, a camera, and Anna's ever present tablet of yellow lined paper for taking notes. We arrived at the VA home about eleven a.m. and spent forty-five minutes with Andy James before he was wheeled away for lunch.

We both noticed the resemblance. Roberta has his dark eyes, and even though he is old, we could see the strong jawline they share. For the first several minutes, he said only a few words to us—nothing close to a complete sentence. Then he suddenly seemed to warm up and became chatty, even charming, though we knew he would not remember a moment of our small conversation.

Andy . . . a nickname given to him by his grandparents. Short for Andre, son of Jeanette and Martin. Andre James, orphaned at three, spent the next fifteen years of his life with Abel and Edna James, his father's dutiful—if not loving—parents. His memories of his mother and sister faded, and he grew to be a handsome, restless teenager. On his eighteenth birthday, his grandparents handed him a journal penned by his mother during the last year of her life. It was the only thing they had kept of hers, and had they bothered to read it, they likely would have burned it. Having been schooled by nuns, Jeanette's penmanship was perfect, and Andre's two years of high school French were put to a test. I excerpt and translate here:

June 17, 1919—The baby is still sick. She cries a lot and has fever. I am also ill.

June 19, 1919—Andre and I are changed forever. Rose cried so much last night. Andre tried to comfort her with blankets. Too many blankets. I should have been watching, but I was sick and fell asleep. Oh my darling Rose. I could not keep you safe, even from your sweet brother. Now you are with the angels. What shall I say? I am afraid. I am so alone.

June 20, 1919—Rose rests here forever. Andre is unaware of his deed. He asks for his sister. I say she has disappeared. I tell everyone she has disappeared. God have mercy. I shall endure this lie for a long time. Beloved Andre, God be with you.

"Andy" had spent the day after his eighteenth birthday reading the journal and realized in these final entries that in his effort to warm his baby sister, he had quite possibly suffocated her. At eighteen he could not comprehend the innocence of his actions, nor could he talk to his grandparents. He became sullen and angry, and he itched to leave the small town that had shunned his mother and offered him little promise of a useful life.

Overwhelmed, Andy packed a duffle bag and told his grandparents he was going to hitchhike and try to work his way across the country before he headed to junior college in the fall. His drift lasted several months, during which he fell in and out of love with several girls and stole pocketbook money from those he managed to spend the night with. When he passed by historic Fort Garland in Colorado, the idea of military service suddenly seemed a good next step. He wired his grandparents, who were relieved to hear from him and delighted that he had chosen such a patriotic career.

He was shot weeks later by friendly fire during maneuvers, perhaps the result of his newly developed streak of self-destruction.

His wound apparently healed quickly, and within a short time, Andy was on a ship bound for the Pacific Islands. He had developed a reputation for being headstrong and courageous, which, outside of military life, would likely have been called foolhardy and impetuous. Whatever the description, Andy was captured at some point and held for a few years. When he was released, he shelved his medals for bravery, excused himself from the service, worked his way back to Grand Rapids and faded into oblivion. He was eventually diagnosed as depressed and suicidal by a doctor who did rounds once a week at a men's shelter. After reviewing his military record, a nurse realized he was eligible for care in the VA hospital, which is where he lived for many years, and where Roberta found him, days after her mother's death.

Eve Marino was beautiful. At least that's what everybody said. Actually, they said she was too pretty for her own good. She modeled clothes at a department store in Grand Rapids and took night classes so she could become a hairdresser. She had inherited her mama's loopy raven curls and black eyes, and among a sea of blond, fair-skinned Dutch girls, Eve stood out like a rare dark pearl.

At nineteen, Eve was voluptuous, curious and tired of being a good girl. She was visiting her aunt Violetta in Omaha when she met up with Andy James, a wanderer from near her hometown, who was having a beer in a downtown bar and hoping to get lucky. Discovering they had grown up about sixty miles apart seemed reason enough to hook up for a while—an adventure that required Andy to shinny up a cedar tree planted too close to Aunt Violetta's house, tiptoe across the roof of the sunporch and slide quietly through an open window into Eve's bedroom.

"He spent a week with Eve," Roberta told us. "She hid him under the bed or in the closet by day, brought him food and slept with him at night. When he left, he handed her a tattered, leather-covered diary and told her it had been his mom's. He asked that she keep it for him and that he would pick it up when they both returned to Michigan."

Eve had managed to turn Andy's head just long enough to get pregnant. Months later, back in Grand Rapids, her bulging tummy was eventually noticed by her mother as more than the result of a hearty appetite. Despite weeks of threats from her banker-father, Eve never confessed her lover's name. Eve was tough. She dropped out of school and got a job so she could support her new baby, named her Roberta and decided it would be best if she put Andy James behind her. And mostly, she did.

Years later, Eve saw Andy's name on a list of new residents at the VA, which the church ran in its bulletin once a month. She never contacted him. Since the old diary he had given her for safekeeping was in French, she had never read it and had long forgotten where she stashed it.

Eve raised Roberta to be independent and capable. Roberta knew from a young age that she had abilities to see and hear things that others didn't, and considered them gifts to be shared carefully. She never asked about her father, and Eve never offered information, until she was dying, not of old age as she had planned, but from a cancer that was late in being caught and spreading quickly. Before it worked its way to her brain, Eve asked Roberta if she might like to know a little about her roots. And her father.

After Eve died, Roberta found the diary among her mother's possessions, drove to the home of a friend who spoke French and implored her to read it aloud.

Spirits don't lie. Jeanette had likely tried for decades to get the succession of residents in Maple Hill to find baby Rose and bury her properly. When Roberta showed up at the house, Jeanette finally had an ear—someone who could actually hear her wishes. And not just someone, but a granddaughter she didn't know she had. It took a while for Roberta and Jeanette to recognize their connection to each other and to Andre, the tired old man at the VA known as Andy, whom Roberta began visiting after her mother died.

And for the first time Roberta could remember in her entire life, she had lied. Big.

She told us she felt that Andre had suffered more than his share, and she was afraid that if she told us the truth, his terrible story would be exposed, and he would have to live it all over again—only this time, in the public eye. She couldn't let that happen, not even for Jeanette, her grandmother.

"When I realized who Jeanette was, and I grasped her request, I tried to reason with her," Roberta explained. "You know, communicating with a spirit is not like talking on the phone. It's subtle. It's full of imagery and impressions. When I told Jeanette about her fragile son, I implored her to move on and leave the past alone. It was over. No one had been hurt by the story she had woven. And Rose had long since transitioned to her next life. I thought I had her convinced. I thought she would leave you alone. I also was pretty sure that your search would be fruitless, and you'd eventually tire of it or move."

And perhaps Jeanette could have ended her crusade, except that Anna and I had actually found someone we thought was Rose's match. And then the hair sample arrived. Letting the old lie die was one thing. But our finding so much "evidence" to support it was, apparently, more than our disquieted spirit could accept. Jeanette had gathered wind and fire, caused the earth to tremble and poured herself into Anna one last time.

The coroner said his investigation of Rose's remains would take a few weeks, and then she could be buried. He was not interested in getting this story on the evening news anymore than we were. "Tragic . . ." I remember him saying, when we explained the circumstances, minus Jeanette's intervention over the past year. "A sad and private family matter." Rose got one small article in a Friday paper that mentioned the exhumed remains of an infant buried for nearly one hundred years in the crawl space of a house. No foul play was indicated.

We had hoped to convince Andy that Rose's death was a terrible accident, and that it's likely she would have died soon from the flu anyway. By all reports, she was a very sick baby. But Andre no longer worried about Rose. Or anything else. He lived in a world known only to himself. Our brief visit revealed that much. He was Rose's closest blood relative, but not capable of choosing her final resting place. Next in a very short line was Rose's niece. Roberta.

She picked a spot in an old cemetery along the lakeshore, long forgotten and visited by few except those who come in the fall to rake leaves and to reattach the tops and bottoms of brittle old headstones. The bushes are overgrown, and little is known about many who are buried there. Roberta believes Jeanette may have been one of them. She has no evidence, only a feeling. And so, just before sunset on the vernal equinox, with only John and me and a solitary cardinal to witness, she opened the plastic box that contained the meager handful of Rose's ashes, tossed them into the wind and let them scatter across the sacred ground. It may have been my imagination, but I believe I heard the earth sigh.

Acknowledgments

As I sit here in the house that inspired this story and think back over the more than ten years since I began writing it, sweet memories of dozens of friends and members of my family float gently through my mind. Writing is mostly a solitary pursuit, yet there are so many people along the way who help keep the writer writing.

Hillary's village raises children. Mine raises writers.

Thank you, Mother, for every word of encouragement you've offered. Thank you for coming to live with us and for waking up wanting to hear what I had written the night before. You knew this genre long before I did, and I loved surprising you with new twists.

Thank you, Papa, for all the golf balls you've left in my path. They help me feel your presence.

Thank you, Paul, for love, patience, and faith. Nothing in recent years has given me so much pleasure as to look up from my computer and tell you, "It's done!"

Thank you, Nancy. I know you don't favor fiction, so your enthusiasm has been especially dear. Now please get me some signing parties in NYC, ok?

Thank you, Ellen, my editor at the University of Michigan Press, for graciously agreeing to read the first twenty pages and then asking for the rest. Thank you for pushing and pulling at all the right times. I love working with you. Thank you to everyone at the Press who helped move this from loose pages to bound book and into the hands of readers. You do good work.

Thank you, Rodney, for inspiring me with your own success as a writer. And if you want to turn this into a screenplay, that's OK with me . . .

Thank you, Bryan and Marc, for using your Book Nook and Java Shop in Montague to showcase and promote writers.

Thank you, Sharon, for taking my very rough idea and turning it into the cover I saw in my mind. Art is magic to me, and you are a master magician.

Thank you to every friend who sat still and let me read excerpts. Thank you for each laugh, each "wow," every "When is it coming out?" You kept me typing. Thank you to the few to whom I dared send pages. Your suggestions made this a better book.

Thank you to everyone who has asked about this book over the past decade. See, if you take forever to complete a manuscript and you talk about it frequently, there are a huge number of people who eventually ask about its progress, and, in my case, offer kind words before rolling their eyes. If not for all of you, this book would likely be nothing more than a really great partially finished story stuck away in an old laptop.

To family and friends, and to you, dear reader opening this book for the first time, may all the voices you hear echoing through your walls be as loving, encouraging, and inquisitive as those I have heard for the past ten years.